Going Down EASY

A Rebel Wayfarers MC & Incoherent MC
Crossover Story

Original version previously published in the
TNTNYC *Patched Over* anthology

MariaLisa deMora

Edited by Hot Tree Editing

Proofreading by Whiskey Jack Editing

Photography: Wander Aguiar, Photography

Model: Jonny James

First Published 2019

ISBN 13: 978-1-946738-41-7

DEDICATION

To Kori and Kelsi: Thank you for making me part of the family. This is for Kave and Khan. #HeWillLoveMe

Contents

ACKNOWLEDGMENTS

I initially set out to write about a different couple in this book. My man Gunny had family ties to Louisiana seeing as he's originally from there, and it seemed a logical transition. Sharon being friends with Vanna over in the Florida panhandle and maybe wanting to be closer to Kitt—it all made sense in a very tidy way.

However, you'll note from the synopsis that this story is not about Gunny and Sharon. Oh, sure, they factor in a large way, because that's just how Gunny rolls once he starts talking, but it seems he's firmly settled in the Fort. Immovable.

Thank goodness we'd already brought another member into the fold who was more comfortable with making a transition. Jock and Silly, once they started talking, were a joy to write. Except when they had their heads up their respective asses. Then, they were frustrating.

Still, I like where we wound up. It's been hella fun to see the worlds of the RWMC, IMC, and CoBos slowly meshing together over the past few stories, and now these clubs are firmly aligned. I hope you like the idea, too.

Thanks are in order for a whole bunch of folks, as always, and I appreciate every one of them.

Andrey Behia and Wander Aguair tolerated my frantic, last minute search for a particular image of Jonny James (the gorgeous model on the cover) and came through with flying colors. You men are wonderful, and I love you.

Becky Johnson and the folks at Hot Tree Editing, you happily tackled the chore of running two different edits simultaneously, one for the original version in the anthology and one for this longer, expanded cut. The result is perfection. Thank you.

Mel from Whiskey Jack Editing: I learn more from you each time we work together. Thank you for your patience, your mentorship, and above all the level-headed alliance you've offered.

To the readers: The publishing bit of this gig is all you. If you read and tell me what you think, I write. It's a weird but true factoid that my creativity is tightly tied to each message, email, and most especially the reviews you leave to spread the word about these characters we all love so much. Thank you, from the bottom of.

To Keegan: You need to go to Sturgis, my man.

Woofully yours,

~ML

Going Down Easy

Former Marine Jacob Tinney found a new life within the Rebel Wayfarers MC in Fort Wayne. The club's members took in Jacob, known as Jock, watched over him as their own, and sustained him with reasons to hold his PTSD at bay for another day.

Into this good life sashayed Silly, Sylvia Perez, a quirky tattoo artist, friend of the club, and woman who hid so much of herself behind a façade. Jock was first intrigued, then enamored, and finally, consumed with lust—and love.

But when Silly is offered the chance of a lifetime to run her own tattoo shop down near the Big Easy, there's little he can do except tell her goodbye. Until an unexpected suggestion comes his way.

What if he could keep the brotherhood of a club, the camaraderie he needed, and transfer that to another patch?

Could he leave the RWMC and patch over?

I Have An Offer

Jock

The mattress shifting woke him. Not an abrupt jostle, more a slow slide of movement followed by a period of stillness. Of waiting.

Jock blinked into the darkness and turned to see a slim silhouette standing next to the bed. This petite wisp of a form was lean, curved in all the right places, and topped by a head of hair he knew was unruly, virtually untamable, just like its owner.

"Sil?" Voice heavy and slow, he drawled out her name as he reached out, fingers stretching until he encountered bare flesh. He stroked down across her knuckles, then up, and finally curved his grip to hold tight to her wrist. "Silly, woman, it's early. Where the fuck you going?"

Jock tugged gently, and she gave gracefully, as she did everything, easing closer until she sat next to his hip, legs curled underneath her naked ass. The glimmer from her phone's screen lit her face from underneath, but even that eerie angle couldn't hide the sheer beauty of her features. She leaned in, and reflections sparkled from the piercings in her eyebrow, her ears. Even her chest and hands held sparks of fire in the night.

"Jock." Her accented croon of his name was worthy of attention, and he gave her that, staring into the shadows of her face until he found the glint of her eyes, fixed on him. With just that, only his name from her lips, his cock was well on its way back to half-mast. Heat settled on his chest, her hand flattened over his heart, and he lifted his head to capture her mouth.

Hot and wet, her tongue teased at the edges of his lips until he sucked it in with a growl. Feeding on her whimpers, he kept the kiss going, renewing it every time it threatened to flag, hand tangled in that crazy hair holding them together until they both were panting for breath.

Jacob "Jock" Tinney, former Marine, current member of the Rebel Wayfarers MC, and bike mechanic at a shop the club owned, was deeply in love with the woman who'd tried to slip from his bed in the middle of the night.

He'd met Sylvia Perez, also known as Silly, at a club party back before he'd been a prospect. She'd approached him, which was the only way it would have happened, given how tangled he'd been in his head at the time. PTSD had been an everyday enemy, and he'd barely been finding his feet in a new town, with new friends. Silly had been confident, quirky, and gorgeous as fuck. He'd been astonished when she'd propped herself at his side with a quick joke, then intrigued when she forced conversation until it wasn't stilted or forced anymore. He'd followed her to a bar where she'd talked about herself, her job, her friends, asking his input on minor things, laughing with him at his more absurd suggestions.

The transition had been so seamless he hadn't realized when they'd gone from talking about her to talking about him. Once he'd been comfortable with that, she'd turned her chocolate brown eyes on him and with a slow blink opined that he could visit her hotel room that night. He'd stood, stunned, until she rolled her plush bottom lip between her teeth and shared that such a visit would not be unwelcome. Liquid courage had bolstered him, and he'd agreed.

That first weekend, she'd put in time exploring his mind, turning him inside out with her puzzles and questions. He'd started out by exploring her body, taking her at her word when she'd claimed all she'd wanted was a good time. After two nights, she'd gone back to Chicago where home and work was, and he'd remained in Fort Wayne, still stumbling through figuring himself out.

What was intended to be wetting his dick in a one-night stand with a friend of the club he was interested in had instead turned into a fifteen-month journey together. Tonight they were in the Fort, in the single room he rented from Domino, one of his brothers, and when she'd arrived without warning, the one fact he'd gotten from her was her work was covered all weekend, which meant he had been promised another three nights with her. Arriving on Friday, she stayed through to Tuesday morning, without fail. So her slipping out of bed, phone in hand, wasn't in line with any of that, and he wanted to know why.

When he finally released her mouth, she collapsed dramatically onto his chest, forcing out an "oof" from him that made her giggle. Cheek to his chest, she drew patterns along his skin with her fingernails, ghost touches interspersed with tiny, burning scratches. Each line drawn by her nails would connect to form a greater whole. Even at rest, her creative soul was always busy, always ready for the next idea, the next tattoo or piercing, the next drawing or canvas, because her art wasn't restricted to flesh.

"Now, tell me where you were going, Silly." He ran a hand slowly up her back, pausing at every dip between her vertebrae, circling the wings of her scapula, and continuing until he could cup her neck in his palm. She settled against him a little more with every moment that passed, arching into the touch like a cat even as she snuggled her cheek into the curve of his shoulder. "Because it's fuckin' early, and you said I had you for the weekend."

She lay quietly until the bare silence rang in his ears. Finally, he heard the sound of her lips parting, and then she softly said, "I have an offer."

"For me?" He blinked into the darkness, frowning. *What the fuck does she mean?*

"No, Jock. I, as in *me*, have an offer I'm considering. It was..." She trailed off for a breath. "It's been weighing on my mind. I was restless, so thought I'd do my thinking quietly on the couch instead of waking you. But here we are." Rolling her head, she planted a kiss against his chest. "With you awake."

"Baby, you can't sleep, you wake me up." He shrugged and chuckled. "I'll put you back to sleep the fun way." She didn't respond to the amusement he'd tried to convey, so he tried a different tactic. "What's the offer? Something good?" Still aiming for humor, he put on a bad New Jersey accent. "Is it an offer you can't refuse?"

Jock didn't have to see her face to know the eye roll she returned. Her giggle, though brief, told him he was breaking through whatever funk had her in its grip. "Something like that, yes."

"What is it? Now you got me goin', Sil. I wanna know." He wrapped his other arm around her, draped his hand just above her round ass, then stroked his palm down a few inches and back up. "Tell me about this mysterious offer."

"Nothing's certain, yet." She sounded hesitant, which was out of character for Silly, and he struggled to keep his breathing steady, waiting.

A sense of impending doom curled in close, and he tried to push it back with mental effort, shoving down the thoughts of "not me" and "no good" and "why bother" that hovered along the edges of his thoughts, always.

His PTSD was the best it had ever been, flashbacks and episodes further and further apart until he didn't have to hold his breath waiting for the next one to strike and fuck him up. But the mood swings and anger, those were harder to harness, even with the meds he was willing to take. *I just need to give her time to tell whatever it is her own way.*

"Okay." He prompted her gently. "So you got things up in the air?"

"Yes, exactly that, Jock. Up in the air." Her fingertip drawing had flowed over to his arm and down his bicep. She soothed them both with the action, and knew it, knew he'd never negate the chance to have her hands on him in any way. "The offer, it would be a big change. So I told them...him, I needed time."

"Him?"

Jock didn't have a chance to hide the edge in his voice. For fifteen months, they'd been exclusive, but if she was going to play him, he'd dump himself from her life fast.

Faster than my old lady did.

He'd cycled stateside from a mission on a lightning-fast round of leave, spending scarcely a weekend at home before having to jump back into the sandbox for nearly a year. Two months in, she'd told him she was pregnant, and Jock had been over the moon. They'd video chatted during every doctor's visit he could arrange, and she'd thrilled him with images of their child, his child, still protected in her womb, waiting to take his first breath. He'd beaten his chest and crowed, because it was a boy, a son, someone to carry on his legacy. That excited high had lasted seven months.

Out of the blue, he'd gotten papers. She was divorcing him. She'd gone into labor and birthed the boy. His wife, now his ex, had cheated on him while he was deployed. The child hadn't been his but her lover's, and Jock had been left to twist in the wind, losing everything he loved in the space of a typewritten letter.

So Silly saying "him" wasn't ever going to sit very well with Jock.

"Who's 'him'?" He shoved up the mattress, Silly rearing up and away from him in shock at his reaction. He knew it was out of proportion to her soft words, but he didn't give that first fuck. Back flat against the painted surface of the wall, he levered into a sitting position, pushing away from her. "What 'him' would this be, Sylvia?" The darkness pressed in against him, and the smell of spilled fuel was overwhelming in the heat of the desert. He blinked, closing his eyes tightly as he shook his head. *No, not now.*

"*Jock.*"

Airy and light, her exclamation didn't register. Jock was three steps ahead in his mind, imagination drawing pictures of her underneath some man. Someone not scarred, torn by war, someone who hadn't gotten his entire unit killed because he'd been fixated on the idea of his wife fucking another man and stealing the chance of his son away.

"*Jock, it's nothing like that.*"

Silly, smiling at someone not him. There were sounds from far away, urgent words strung together that didn't make sense.

"I'd never do that to you."

Silly, gorgeous and glowing, determination on her shining face as she worked to bring a child to air. Her hand clutched a man's, ring glinting against her dark skin.

"Jock, come back to me."

A man who wasn't him, could never be him, because why would she settle? Woman like her, she didn't have to. He'd known that all along, since he'd watched the most beautiful woman he'd ever seen cross a room to stand beside him. "I'm silly," she'd said, and he'd laughed.

"Jock, you're with me, here. We're here."

Squirming weight wiggled into his lap until he could feel the warmth plastered all along his chest, her unique comfort blanketing him, that gorgeous, painted skin touching his, smooth as silk, fingers cradling his head. Her. *Silly.*

"Jake, baby. Come back to me."

Urgent and afraid, the tone finally dug through, raising an alarm. Covered with clammy, sticky sweat, he blinked, eyes scratchy and dry. Sylvia stared at him, face close enough to share breath. "Jake." Her mouth moved, and he nodded. Relief flooded her features, and he watched her lids sweep closed, long dark lashes brushing the curve of her cheek before she opened her eyes again, and all he could see was the warm, chocolatey brown beauty shining up at him. "Jock, baby. You scared me."

Mouth clamped shut, he pulled in a hard, deep breath that seemed to go on and on. When his lungs were full, near to bursting, he hitched his chest and forced in a bit more, then held it until it burned hot at the back of his throat. Until the muscles of his back were jumping and jerking, trying to expel the air, useless and all used up, nothing left to sustain life. *Like me*, he thought as he let it rush out of him, poison flowing over his lips.

"I'm sorry." God, he hated those words. Meaningless when overused, they stained the air around him constantly. *Sorry* for failing. *Sorry* for being the man he'd turned into. *Sorry* for panicking. *Sorry* for breaking. Sorry for *breathing*, some days. The only ones he didn't feel that way with were Silly and his brothers in the RWMC. And now he'd broken that streak, here in bed with her, by flipping out over something he knew he'd concocted inside his own head. "I'm sorry."

"No sorries, baby." She covered his mouth with her hand, head shaking back and forth firmly as she reminded him of her rule. "No sorries. Not with me."

His PTSD might be better, but it would never be gone. And she knew, of course she knew. He'd told her as much not a month ago when she'd come in unexpectedly to find him curled into the corner of the room, shaking, caught inside the memories of the night his unit had died. *She could do so much better.*

Silly pushed past his silence. "This is on me. My timing was shit, but I'm tired and anxious, and you were so beautiful waking up like that. If you're *with* me, I'll tell you everything. This wasn't me trying to keep secrets. Not from you. Never from you. And never that. I'd sooner cut off my own hand than do something to hurt you. But if you're with me, I'll talk. Are you with me? Jock? Are you?"

"Yeah, Silly. I'm with you." He shrugged, feeling the skin of his back catch on the chilly bedroom wall. The surface of the burns he'd suffered wasn't smooth there but pitted. Rough. Damaged. *Like me.* "I wasn't, but I am now."

"The man I work for, you know him, no?" His trembling smile at her convoluted language failed before it hit his lips, so he just nodded. "He runs the shop, and owns it. You know he owns a bunch more, too. He got noticed a few years back, because of who and what he does. When he first opened the shop, he had to have a friend file the paperwork."

"Mason." Jock had heard this story a few times. "The previous club's president thought he owned your boss and yanked him around, hard. Mason was part of it, but not party to it, if that makes sense, because he'd battled his own president over it."

"Yes." Silly's expression grew earnest, intense. "The *pendejo* he was, he demanded free while keeping profits from anything Ernesto did. Working out of basement rooms, in kitchens, he did tats for all the Fiends while trying to earn enough to go legit."

"When Mason took over the club and reformed it, he went back and righted a bunch of things he'd felt were wrongs done. Backing the shop however he could was one of them." Jock slipped sideways, toppling them both back to the mattress, and curled around Silly, touching his forehead to hers. "At the time, it was something legal, right?"

"*Si*. Local laws prevented felons from owning undesirable businesses by limiting necessary licensing. An antiquated law, but on the books, and enforced by those who didn't want unwelcome influence in their space. Tattoo parlors require multiple licenses to exist, along with bars, strip clubs, pawn shops." She rolled her eyes, and he smiled. "So Ernesto made it his mission to educate people and change the laws. The day the law's repeal became official, Mason handed over paperwork that put the shop in Ernesto's name. The next day, Ernesto opened a second shop, and a national magazine ran a story. Then he got interviewed all over the country, because these kinds of laws are still everywhere. Then he got a shot at the show."

"You are hot as fuck on that show." Same eye roll, and his grin was broader, wider, more real. "No joke, Silly. Watching you work on all those people, doesn't matter their background, who they are, what they own, how much power or control they have in their own lives—they get in your chair or on your table, and you fuckin' own them." She stared into his eyes, unblinking. "Hot. As. Fuck."

"Whatever." She brushed her lips against his. "I was pleased for him, because he'd earned that chance to grow the business. And he has. By leaps and bounds, he opened shops in the hometowns of all the winners, set them up to work for him for a year. Smart business, that. The show gave them so much exposure their books were full when the doors opened for the first time. No slow rise to the top through word of mouth. He's got almost twenty shops now, all over."

"So many? I didn't know." He whistled low. "That's why he's always stressed. Man lives on energy drinks, swear to God."

"He opened one near New Orleans two years ago. Big splash. Famous tattoo guy coming to the Big Easy and making his mark." She shrugged. "Only problem is, the winner was all flash and no staying power. He lasted the contracted year, but no more. They'd taken over an existing shop, too, so the other tattoo artists will be impacted if Ernesto has to close it."

"Sucks, baby." Jock cupped her cheek, then pushed to thread his fingers through her hair. Tangled from sleeping, the strands slipped through his hands until they were even again. "Can't he just have one of the other guys run it instead?"

"He wants me, Jock. That's the offer. He wants to hand me my own shop. Established, and already profitable—he wants me to take it over."

"New Orleans is a fuck of a lot farther from the Fort than Chicago." The words were out before he could school his tongue, and he saw her flinch. *Dammit. I'm a fucking asshole.* "Shit, baby. What I meant to say is that's huge. It's a huge honor for you. Says how much the man trusts you. I'm proud." He pulled in a slow, even breath, trying to beat back the wings of panic that threatened to choke him.

New Orleans wasn't a five-hour commute. It was a full day and a half driving, or a flight. The idea of getting into another plane had more sweat prickling the back of his neck in seconds. New Orleans didn't host an RWMC chapter, not anywhere near there. Their Memphis chapter had been abandoned, and that left Little Rock, or somewhere in Kentucky he hadn't been to yet. The club had friends all along the coast, sure, but not a single RWMC chapter to be found.

He steeled himself and looked at Silly without trying to hide his love for her for once. She'd told him early on that he couldn't get attached. She had some fucking rule about never falling in love, and he'd jokingly promised her if it happened, she'd never know. He'd kept that promise until today, right here, in his bed, when he told her with everything inside him what she'd come to mean to him. Silently, stuffing down the pain already blooming in his gut at losing her.

"You're going to do great."

***

Silly

She lay next to Jock. Head nestled on the pillow and Jock's hip and leg angled over her thighs, pressing her deep into the mattress. They hadn't started out this way. She'd been cuddled into his side, his arm holding her in place against him. But Jock had evidently internalized her attempt to slide from bed earlier, and now, even in his sleep, was ensuring she stayed right where she was.

In the year and a half she'd known him, almost all of that building towards a deeper relationship, she'd done every second of it with eyes wide open. She'd heard the stories about the man Gunny had adopted as near family, how he'd bonded with Gunny and

Brute, even more of the RWMC, but mostly with the men who had served.

Slate was someone she considered one of her closest friends, and he'd been the one to nudge her Jock's way that first night. With that confidence bolstering her, she'd been clear to make a direct approach and had never regretted an instant. In moments, she'd been curious, then attracted, and finally blown away by the man's intellect and sense of humor.

With the stress of work, life hadn't seemed easy for a long time, but something about Jock made everything effortless. It wasn't that he didn't make demands of her or didn't challenge her, but the way he did it showed his respect for and faith in her in every way. When someone believed in a person like that? Everything else smoothed out.

Then Ernesto had thrown a monkey wrench into everything. He'd approached her Wednesday as she sat sketching on the table in her station, waiting on her next appointment to show. Blunt as always, something she'd always appreciated, he'd laid it out fast, in broad strokes, knowing she'd need the whole picture before she could get into the details.

"Need you, Silly. Place is holding on by a fingernail, but it has the potential to be one of the most profitable shops." Ernesto rolled back and forth on the stool he'd brought in with him. "I could shuffle folks,

but it'd be takin' a good manager from a shop and replacing them with one not as good. You've never been official, but we all know you're the one who keeps things running smooth here."

That wasn't a lie. She'd spent two hours the previous night upgrading their bookkeeping software to keep it on the same version as the other shops. Then she'd spent another hour tallying the needed supplies. She'd shown up an hour early today to place those orders. Ernesto did the hiring, but he had her interview every artist or other employee. She ran the shop, except in name.

"When do you need an answer?" He'd looked shocked, then stared at her with narrowed eyes. "Jesus, Ernie, you couldn't have expected I'd just leap for joy and say yes, did you?" Pursed lips joined the narrowed eyes to complete the scowl. "You did. I'm honored, truly, but I've got a life, and that life isn't in Louisiana."

"Man wants to be with you, he'd make that happen." This was something Ernie had been grumbling about for the past couple of months. Treating Silly like a daughter extended to vetting her romantic partners—the long-term ones, anyway. She'd only had one of those before, and Ernie hadn't liked him. His dour pronouncements about the man's lack of commitment had proven correct, something she found out when she walked into the guy's

apartment using the key he'd given her to find him sleeping next to a nude blonde. "If Jock wanted to shift to any of the Chicago chapters, Mason'd greenlight that without pause. The fact he hasn't even asked, Sil, that says something."

"He wasn't a prospect when I met him. Fury held him to a nine-month recruit period. He's been a patched member less than a year, Ernie. You and I both know he's putting in the time, like he should. You'd be pissed if he wasn't doing that." His scowl deepened and she barked a short laugh. "Your face is gonna freeze that way."

"You'll give it real consideration?" He leaned back, muscles in his thighs pushing and pulling, rocking the stool back and forth. "Won't reject me out of hand?"

"Of course. That's what I'm trying to do right now." She reached out and wrapped her fingers around his, lifting and shaking his hand. "Love you hard, old man. I'm honored, and that's no lie. But I have to wrap my head around what it means."

"Love you like my own, Sylvia." Ernesto had heavy features, dark and thick brows, a nose that had been broken more times than she had fingers on a hand, and a scar tracing up his neck and across one cheek. Family and friends said his time spent in what he called con college had hardened him, but all Sylvia saw when she looked at him was the sweet man who'd taken a chance on a girl who could sketch, giving her a

seat at his side and an opportunity to apprentice with a master.

"I know you do." She shook his hand again and released him as the bell over the door sounded. "That's my next appointment."

Jock hadn't been able to hide his pain when she'd told him. Not the setting she'd have chosen, but even forced by circumstances, she'd tried to tell him without saying it that if he asked her to stay, she would. She should have delayed the conversation somehow, because with him on the tail end of that episode, she knew in her gut he couldn't have made a decision about what to order for dinner.

The first time she'd seen him fraying like that, he'd beaten it back, putting on a stoic face. They'd been at a local bar shooting pool when the guys at a table three over had dropped their tray of balls. The rapid smacking of the hard balls against the bare concrete floor had been loud, overwhelming, and when she'd looked to Jock, she initially couldn't find him. After a moment, she saw him crouched low at the end of the table, and when he finally unfolded upright, she hadn't missed how pale his face was. Leaning over the table to take her next shot, she got his attention with a tiny bit of bared cleavage, something she'd noticed early on he liked, rolled her eyes, and said with a head tip towards the rowdy table, "Idiots. Let's finish this one and go back to your place."

The next time had been more pronounced. Down in Fort Wayne to visit him a week later, on her last night in town she'd left to pick up supper for them, intending to eat in bed before talking him into fucking her, not usually something she had to try hard for, a fact she liked because it said a lot about how he felt around her. Their first time he'd been hesitant to show his scars, but her matter-of-fact handling of them seemed to soothe his nerves, and it hadn't been long before his manner told her they no longer factored in his mind when she was around.

She'd gotten back, said hey to Domino, who'd been sprawled on the couch in the shared space of the living room, and danced her way into Jock's room. It had been dark, which was startling, but when she flipped the lights on, he'd started yelling, screaming at her to turn them off, because "they" would see and everyone would die. It had only been a moment until she'd felt Domino at her back, and even before approaching Jock, he'd made a call to Gunny. Ten minutes later, Gunny and Brute were in the room, she was on the couch, and the food had been growing cold on the kitchen table.

Hours had passed, growling murmurs rattling Jock's door, Silly waiting and not sure what to do. Then the outside door opened and Slate walked in. "Come on, honey." He'd wrapped an arm around her. "Ruby's got a bed made up for you."

The next weekend she'd come back down, an out-of-cycle visit, but she couldn't stand not seeing him. All conversations that week had been short, and he'd seemed tired, exhausted, never mentioning what had happened. That continued, and his shock at seeing her hadn't been feigned, nor had his gleeful excitement or the way he'd immediately gone about rescheduling anything he'd needed to spend the time with her. She hadn't pushed, and at the end of the weekend, she'd made a stop on her way out of town. Slate had answered the door, swept her into a hug, and at her choked question, smiled sadly. "He won't remember."

She'd seen more episodes, none of them that extreme, and never, not once, had she felt endangered. The incidents had dwindled, seemingly in direct relation to how much time they spent together, until she was making regular trips down every other week. He'd come to Chicago sometimes, too, hanging out with his patch brothers there while she worked.

Through it all, they'd grown closer every time they were together, until she couldn't imagine her life without him in it. But now, with Ernesto's offer, and with Jock's seemingly easy acceptance of her imminent exit from his life, she'd have to.

***

21

"Ernesto called." She kept her back to him as she lifted her bag to the bed, folding and placing the clothes she'd worn yesterday inside. "He set a meeting with the bank to officially get me on the accounts, but I have to be there to sign papers and stuff. He's been meaning to do it for months, but we kept putting it off." She shrugged. "Saves me from signing his name on orders and stuff."

Not a lie; she'd never do that to Jock. She'd also not tell him that Ernie had offered to delay the appointment, knowing she'd be home early on Tuesday. Right now it was Monday morning, and Jock was expecting her to be here another night. Every other weekend, she showed on Friday and didn't pull out headed for Chicago until just before sunup four days later.

"It's Monday." Jock's voice was gruff in his surprise.

"Yeah, I know." She zipped the bag and glanced around the room to verify she hadn't left anything behind. Not something she'd worried about before, and she knew he'd pick it up as a difference. "There's a lot to think about, talk about." Slinging the strap over her shoulder, she turned, startled to find him directly behind her. Angling her chin up, she caught his gaze. "I have a lot of thinking to do."

"You can't do that here?" The hurt in his voice set up a resonance in her chest, making the back of her throat tight with echoed ache. He stared into her eyes, a heavy line appearing between his brows. Absently, he lifted a hand and ran his fingers across her cheek, fingertips gliding towards her ear, where she felt a light, fleeting touch along the gems of her earrings. "With me?"

Silly let her eyes slip closed, shutting out the vision of Jock's face, ravaged with pain. "I just...I need some time, Jake."

His touch didn't falter, sweeps of his thumb along her skin, and she lifted her chin when his other hand hit her throat, soft and gentle, a glide up to cup her cheeks between his palms. His breath trailed over her lips an instant before his mouth covered hers, the kiss starting slow and measured, and when she would have pushed it, taking it further, he kept it controlled. Soft, sweet, and so damned gentle, but that didn't take from the intensity. His quivering breaths told her he wasn't far from losing himself, and she knew that to be true when he broke away suddenly and wrapped her up tight, arm around her shoulders, hand holding her cheek to his chest.

"Okay, Sylvia." His heart was pounding, and Silly clutched the sides of his shirt under his vest, holding just as tight. "Okay."

***

She stopped at Slate's on her way out of town, knocking at the side door, and as he always did, when her friend answered and saw her red-rimmed eyes, he didn't ask any questions, just pulled her in close for a hug while dragging her back inside his house.

"Ruby, I'll be in the office with Silly." A woman's voice responded from somewhere deeper in the house, where Silly could hear the chiming voices of children.

He moved them to that office, put her ass in a chair, and brought her two fingers of whiskey in a glass he wiped at with his sleeve. Then he sat down at the desk, opened a drawer and pulled out a notebook, fired up his computer, and ignored her while he did something, probably club business.

By the time she'd finished sipping the liquor, he angled his head to glance at her. "You ready to talk?" She shook her head. "Need another double?" She gave him a rough smile and again shook her head. "Okay." He turned back to the monitor and started clicking away at the keyboard.

She twisted and placed the glass on a nearby table, the base making a soft clink as she set it down. "Easy as that?"

"Easy as you need it, Silly. Always." He didn't even look away from what he was doing. "Easy as you need."

"Ernie—" She'd barely gotten the name out before Slate scoffed far back in his throat. "Stop. I know you don't like him, but he only refused you the one time. And you were drunk."

"I was not drunk." He angled that look at her again, this time with a tiny smile. "I was inebriated. And I wanted a tattoo."

"You were high as a kite, too."

He shook his head, and she wondered how Ruby stood his stubbornness.

With a sigh that hopefully told him what a pain in the ass he was, she insisted, "Yes, you were. I poured you into a bed in the back of the shop, so I can say that with authority." Silly leveled a stern look at him. "You wanted a monkey's ass tattooed on your belly, using your bellybutton as the asshole because you thought it would be funny. Face it, buddy. We saved you from yourself."

"He still shoulda done it. I was one of his best customers."

She snorted and shook her head. If she hadn't intervened that night, Ernie would have done it, and Slate would have had to live with that for the rest of his life. He knew better.

Pushing back from the desk, Slate folded his arms behind his head, stretched, and told her what he always did when she talked to him about anything. "Tell me."

"Ernie—" she paused a beat to see if he'd interrupt again, but he didn't "—has offered me a shop to take over, run it like it's mine. It's a good gig. The shop is already established, popular, and in a great location. It's got history, and you know that matters to me, and the place is perfect."

"No, it's not." She looked at him, lifting an eyebrow. "If it was perfect, you wouldn't be leading with that weepy-eyed look you knocked on my door with. So let's begin again, and tell me what's not so perfect."

"It's not in Chicago." She swallowed, realizing for the first time that taking this opportunity meant more than losing Jock. It meant losing all the friends she'd made along the way, including this man in front of her. Someone she'd watched and hurt for, back when he'd been looking for something to hang his hat on, and then pleased for him when he found it in Ruby. "It's not in Fort Wayne, or anywhere close." He stared at her, face impassive, but she saw a tiny tic in a muscle along his jaw. "It's near New Orleans."

"That, my dear, is a problem." He leaned forwards, propping his elbows on his knees, wrapped a hand around the back of his neck and muttered, "Fuck me."

"Yeah."

"It's perfect?"

"Yeah, been in the same building since the late eighties, but they've done a bunch of reno in the past couple of years. It's a show shop." He'd know what she meant, being as he not only was an avid watcher of the program but had also wrangled his way into her chair twice during filming, so he was on the show, too. "Gallagher, season six winner, walked out the day after his mandatory contract was up. The lead artist has been holding it together, but it's a strain because he's not business-minded."

Slate considered her a moment, then muttered softly, "Fuck me. You are."

"I am." She lifted a shoulder in a dismissive shrug. "I'm also a talented tattoo artist and am a fair hand at piercing." He snorted and she flipped him off, making him smile briefly. "Shaddup, you. I don't like to toot my own horn."

"Written up in four magazines that I know of. I'd say you're better than talented and a fair hand."

He wasn't exactly wrong, but it was actually seven magazines. *Not the time to correct him.*

Slate stared at her, expression falling into an impassive mask. "So it's perfect."

I hate when he gets like this. She knew he'd be making his point soon, so she held her peace and nodded.

The mask fractured, broke, and he lifted his upper lip in a sneer. "Except for it's what, a thousand miles away?"

"Nine hundred twenty-seven." She sucked in an uneven breath, trying to push down the tears. These were numbers she'd run through her head time and time again, no repeat making them less. "Point seven."

"Fuck, Silly. You're stuck between what you want and what you need." He pushed to his feet and paced around the desk, coming to crouch in front of her. The heat of his hands covering hers were a balm, so comforting and safe it nearly broke her in half. "What'd Jock say?"

The remembered pain from Jock's blurted statement washed through her. "Before or after he had a minute to put a muzzle on himself?" She laughed, but it sounded so jagged she shut her lips tight. *God, why now?*

Slate's thumbs slid along her knuckles, dipping between each in a slow up and down that mimicked her rollercoaster emotions. After a moment he tightened his grip, giving her hands a shake. "I get it. Brother like him? Had a dream taken from him and felt the bite of that? Once he got his head wrapped around it, he'd be all about encouraging you." Slate shook his head, his gaze pained and bright with wet he quickly blinked away. "We all know I'm an asshole. Means my message to you? Always gonna be don't go. But Jock?"

He paused long enough she felt compelled to honesty. "He said I'd do great."

"And you would, if you were going. Which you aren't. Don't go." He rested his chin on his hand, pointing pouting lips up at her. Clearly his tactic had changed to teasing persistence. "Don't go."

She let her head tip to the side as she stared at him. *If only it were that easy.* "It's not decided. I'm headed back to Chicago—"

His grip tightened into a vise that ground her knuckles together. "It's Monday."

Her head rocked back with the force of his words. She stared at the ceiling, finding no peace in the blameless white texture. "*God.* I know what day of the week it is." Looking back at Slate, she saw he'd lost any pretense of humor. "I have to think."

"And if you're doing that anywhere except where you can do it pressed up against Jock to remind yourself why you don't want to go, then you've already decided, Sylvia." He moved his head back and forth in a slow shake. "You're lying to yourself, and that ain't like you."

His words cut too close to the bone, and she'd forgotten how his honesty could hurt. "I gotta go." With a trembling hand, she pushed at her hair, fingers getting tangled in the short mass, and stood. Slate did, too, taking a step backwards to give her some space so he wouldn't loom over her. She laughed softly before she leaned into him for a hug. After getting used to Jock, he didn't seem so big anymore, and she'd found she liked how Jock towered over her.

What do I do?

***

She reached out and smoothed the papers in front of her down the middle, feeling the tiny bumps each line of the contract created. As she would read someone's skin, she spread her fingers edge to edge, mapping the height of the stack by how it compressed in the center.

She'd brought everything Ernesto had given her to Fort Wayne with her, all the info, wedging a fat folder into the bottom of her bag like a bad memory.

Slate's house had gotten loud during her leave-taking, with Ruby and the kids coming out to chat and tell her goodbye. At one point she had a child swinging from each hand, Kayley and Hayley, Slate's youngest girls, alternately jabbering at her, when she looked over at Slate. He was watching the scene, taking in Ruby standing close, bending and automatically taking things from Allen that could be turned into weapons. Dani was pretending to hide behind her mother, dipping out to flash smiles at Silly, who met each approach with a crazy face. The happiness on Slate's face brightened the whole room, face soft, eyes softer, body relaxed. The man loved his wife, adored his kids, and didn't give a shit who saw it. He also loved her, but she'd watched that brightness dim when he glanced at her, his pain and worry eating at that happiness he'd earned.

As he walked her to her car, he'd said, "Think on it long and hard. You've got a really good thing with Jock. You can throw everything else to the curb, but that stands on its own. Fuck, girl. I'll miss you, but I'll come visit and bring the fam. I love you, Silly, but you aren't my life. What you saw inside just now? That's what I live and breathe for." He bent close, brushed his cheek against hers, and whispered pain into her ear. "That's what you are for Jock, honey." He stepped away and closed her door, patting the top of the car. "Think on it," he'd said as she pulled away.

Instead of turning the wheels towards Chicago, she'd called Ernie and rescheduled. Then she went to Jock's place, only to have to use her key to get inside, because no matter that he had cleared his Monday like he always did, he wasn't home now.

So Silly sat on the floor of his bedroom, dining room chair carried in to act as a desk, and prepared to finally read the agreement, cover to cover.

32

Got My Back

Jock

"Pisses me right the fuck off."

Jock rolled his eyes at the loud declaration from directly behind where he sat on a rolling mechanics stool. It was early yet, and he'd had a cup of coffee, but maybe not enough for whatever conversation this was going to be. He'd flicked all the bolts and fasteners he'd removed from the bike earlier into the pan that sat just above the castors, and was in the process of unwedging the back fender from its longtime home on the back frame. Jock's job in the garage was to execute Bear's motorcycle designs, taking what the man drew up in his specifications and recommendations and making them real. Right now, however, his participation wasn't even necessary in this conversation, because Gunny was wound up tight. So tight, he could talk to himself for now without any contribution from Jock.

"I'm telling you, that woman's shit better get sorted. Fast." The last word was hissed, and Jock knew if he turned to look, the expression on his best friend's face would be fierce.

After a lengthy pause, Jock asked, "That woman?"

"My mother-in-law. Shar's mom has it in her head that she has a right to have goddamned input on my boy's name." Fabric shifted, and he imagined Gunny recrossing his legs at the ankle, his normal stance when they were having discussions. "It's my boy. She doesn't have a right to squat."

"She's Sharon's mother."

"She's Canadian."

"Hey." Jock looked up at the annoyed shout from across the bay. Captain stood there, fists on his hips. "I'm Canadian."

"Oh, man. You're fucked." Jock's whispered commentary was directed towards the bike, but knew Gunny'd heard him.

"Who are we talking about? Where's this Canadian you're all up in arms about, eh?" A folder flashed in front of Jock's face, and he jerked backwards, rolling away from the bike and whatever it was Captain was trying to shove in his direction. "Take this, I got a beef with my sister's beau."

"Can't." He held up his hands. "Greasy." The glower Gunny was directing towards Captain wasn't promising. "Lane, man. Remember yourself here." Jase Spencer, also known as Captain, was Gunny's brother-in-law, which could make this little chat even more interesting. "Brothers."

"Your mother"—Gunny started with a bang, and Jock groaned—"thinks she's gonna have a say in the name for my boy."

"Last time I checked, your boy already had a name." Jase drew himself up tall, chin thrust forwards. "And a damn good one, too." Gunny's son, Joshua Wade Robinson, had been named using his father's and uncle's middle names. "One I heartily approved of. If my mom is looking to change that up, she's gonna have to talk to me, first. I got dibs on that boy."

"Fucking hell, man. I ain't talkin' about Josh. Who in their goddamned right mind would change the name of a baby already named and answering to it? Jesus, Jase. I'm talking about the boy Shar's carryin' right now."

Silence from Captain, and to Jock, he seemed frozen. Apparently he hadn't known Sharon was pregnant. Jock knew, but only because the last time he took Tank over to visit, the mastiff had zeroed straight into Sharon's middle, pressing his snout deep into her belly while she cupped the sides of the big dog's head. When she'd looked away, the tears on her cheeks had scared him until she choked out, "He knows. How does he know?" That woman and dog had a history, a connection that went soul deep, and he couldn't give her any answer other than the truth. "He'll always know because he loves you." Gunny and Sharon had adopted Tank when he'd been lost to Jock and had graciously invited him to share in their lives once Jock had found him again. With Tank came Gunny, and with Gunny had come the Rebels.

"Brother? Did I break you?" Gunny's teasing was gentle, something Jock hadn't heard from him often, unless it was directed at his wife or kids. "Jase, you okay, man?"

"She nearly died." At Captain's quietly intense words, Gunny's back went ramrod straight, and he made a choked sound. Slowly, Jock stood from the stool, prepared to get between the two men if needed. "I kept my peace, but this." He groaned, the sound so painful Jock's hair stood on end. "Jesus, Lane. She nearly fucking died, man. That was with Kitten. You had Cadence and it wasn't enough. Kitten, you got your little girl, and seeing you in that hospital,

I thought you'd understand how precious it was to need to hold tight to what you got. But then you pushed, and you got Josh. You have everything a man could ask for in your hands, and you're pushing again? She"—he bent at the waist, throat corded, face red as he shouted"—nearly fucking *died*."

"You think I don't know? You think I don't understand? Her and me, and it's worth sayin' that this is my *wife* you're talking about, we know the risks." The lowered rumble running through his words spoke volumes about how Gunny was restraining himself. "Risks every day, brother. Ridin', workin', hell, anything that involves making a life is risky. Doc said what happened with Kitten was a onetime thing. We checked early on with Josh. No problem. Already checked with this one. Again, no problem. I have my hand on her heart every night, and she's got hers cradled around her belly, because that's the chain of love we have. I nearly lost her, too, Jase. Love my daughters. Love my son. You're in our lives, and you know how deep that is. But if it was a choice?"

Silence hung heavy in the garage, and Jock knew he wasn't the only one paying close attention to this encounter. Gunny unleashed was a force of nature. He'd been the chapter's unofficial enforcer for years, often unasked. Jase was a scrapper, too. Born and bred to the hockey rink, he'd fought bare-knuckled battles of his own, too many to count.

Jase broke the stalemate. Dropping his chin to his chest, he rolled his shoulders as he bowed in the middle, as if with pain. His voice was soft when he answered Gunny's question. "It wasn't." Jase took a step closer, head slowly wagging back and forth. "Praise the saints you didn't have to make a choice. And I was out of line just now." He gripped Gunny's shoulder. "She's my sister first, and always, but she's your heart now. I know you wouldn't risk losing her." He huffed out a soft laugh. "So Ma knew, too?" He looked at Jock. "And you?" Jock nodded. "Where the fuck have I been in all this?"

"Workin' your ass off at the foundation is what I heard. Caught it from DeeDee she hasn't seen you for supper in nearly two weeks, unless she brought it to your office. What's up with that, brother?" Gunny angled backwards and leaned against the work surface, long legs stretched out as if there hadn't nearly been a brawl between two brothers only a moment ago. Jock tried to hide his smirk but knew Gunny caught it when he tossed back a brand of his own.

"One of the coaches quit on me." A long, slow expulsion of air spoke to the level of frustration Jase carried. "I came over to see if you'd help."

"Me?" Gunny scoffed. "Not a skater, dude. Sorry."

"Dammit." Jase flung out one hand. "What if I said all you had to do was coach from the bench? No drills, no ice time."

Now that the confrontation was over, it was time for Jock to step in. "Hoss could help out." Jock watched both their heads swivel towards him. "He's put in the time to learn for Samboni."

"He's already picked up assisting one of the other coaches." Lips pulled thin in a grimace, Jase shook his head. "I tagged him right away when I got wind of stuff going sideways."

Jock considered him. "What went sideways?" Brow furrowed, Jase tightened his mouth. Jock pressed him. "Seriously, brother. What went sideways?"

"I didn't like how he was with the kids. Took him to the side and discussed, thought I'd made my position plain. Realized a week later I hadn't, but only when I overheard some parents talking about a game he'd coached. His methods?" Jase shook his head. "Not cool."

An idea growing in his head, Jock gestured towards his burns from the day everything had gone to shit, hell raining from the sky, the scars he bore on the outside. "You think the kids'll give a shit? What I look like?" Jase's expression turned pained, and Jock persisted, going careful and giving Jase an easy out.

"Like I said. Seriously, brother. You think they'd be put off?"

"You can skate?"

Jock shrugged like it wasn't a big deal, but the idea of helping out with kids was growing on him. *I'll have all that time to fill on the weekends soon.* "It's been a few years, but yeah, I've skated a time or two. I'd be happy to help you out, short term."

Suddenly energized, Jase started bouncing on the balls of his feet. "I don't think the kids will give a shit what you look like, long as you aren't an ass, and I know you, there's not a bit of asshole left in there." He gave a wide grin. "Silly done straightened your act up and filled you full of goodness."

The pain that lanced through Jock wasn't physical, but that didn't mean it couldn't leave a mark. He knew he'd let his hit his face when Jase paused, then said cautiously, "Everything okay with Silly? She's here this weekend, right? I didn't expect to find you in here." He gestured around the garage, filling with brothers and customers, the sound level rising to the point it wouldn't be long before Jock and Gunny fled. That's why they always came in early, to avoid the crush and noise. "Figured you'd be laid up in bed with your sweetness."

"She needed some time." Gut rolling, Jock turned away to grab a rag off the floor by the bike. He bent to gather up the parts still on the metal pan, folding them into the material. Without looking around, he muttered, "Thought I'd get some work done."

"She's not here but a couple days a month." Gunny's voice was as close to incredulous as Jock'd ever heard it, and he glanced up to see the man's expression matched the tone, comically. *I'd laugh if it didn't hurt so much.* "Why the fuck does she need time away from you while she's here?"

"She needed time." He shrugged. Tools gathered, he slotted them back into place in his boxes, dropping the parts into an oil wash that would keep them ready for his next step. He scrubbed his hands at the sink, working the pumice around his nails. "Said it's going to be busy and intense, and she needed time. So I gave it to her."

"Jock, what the fuck is going on?" Jase had moved closer. "You can talk to us, eh?"

"She's got an offer. Ernesto wants her to run one of his shops."

"That's good news, brother. Shop of her own, she'll have more time and money, be a sweeter deal for you." Gunny's hand landed on his shoulder, fingers giving him a squeeze, then dropping away. "Good for both of you."

He swallowed hard, clearing the lump from his throat. As hard as it was to think about, saying it out loud made it real. The words would show his brothers what a sad sack he was, a man who couldn't keep not one, but two women. "In New Orleans." He stretched the sounds as Silly had, making it come out more like New Awlins. "Not Chicago. Not here."

"*Fuck*." Gunny's single word carried all the misery Jock had in his chest.

First one hand, then another landed in the center of his back, directly over his spine. Palms laid flat over the patch he wore, and he understood what it meant. His brothers would stand at his back through this, however it fell out. If Silly stayed, they'd be happy for him. Happy for her, too. If she left to follow the dream of being her own boss, running the show, pushing other artists to see how high they could fly? Well, they'd be at his back then, too.

"Yeap."

***

Slate

"Yo."

Slate greeted the man walking into the clubhouse, his oldest friend. "Mason, brother. Thanks for coming." He stood, reached, and grabbed hold, pulling Mason into a one-armed clinch. His shoulders already felt lighter, just knowing at the end of the conversation there'd be another head working on the same problem. "I got something to lay on ya, see what kind of magic you can pull out of your hat." He settled back into his chair.

"I'm not a magician." Mason chuckled as he took the seat opposite Slate, stretching out his legs with a sigh. "But I *am* a man with an opinion on everything."

"No fuckin' shit, brother." Slate laughed, but it died off fast. The look on Silly's face had haunted his dreams last night, making him even more determined to find a solution for her and Jock's dilemma. "Ernie's hit the big time, you know?"

That earned him a smile, broad and unfettered. "Yeah, man's done all right for himself."

"You set him on that path. I wasn't there, but I heard." Slate looked down and laughed softly. Being on the receiving end of many a Mason Maneuver, as the club called his machinations, he knew how proud the man was when things went according to plan. "Miracle worker."

The weight of Mason's gaze brought Slate's eyes back up, and he let some of his pain shine through. Quietly Mason asked, "First a magician, now a miracle worker? What you need to run past me, brother?"

In for a penny. "Say there was a brother found himself the one, a woman who'd do more than warm his bed, but would be his old lady in every sense of the word. You be happy for the man?" Slate stared at his friend, the man who'd brought him into this life, and waited, knowing there'd be wisdom at the end of their conversation.

"I'd be happy for him." Mason sat up, looking more alert as he propped elbows on his knees. Voice rough with suppressed emotion, he asked, "You got shit goin' on I don't know about, man?"

Shocked, Slate blurted, "What?" It hit him then, what Mason was thinking, and he rushed to reassure his friend. "Me…no, man. No. Me and Ruby's tight. We're good. Golden."

Mason's stare was intense. "Then what's this about?"

"Jock and Silly, man." He shook his head, still not quite believing how something so clearly right and good could be at risk of dying. "Jock and Silly." Slate laid it out for him, and at the end, Mason sat back in his chair and sighed. "*Fuck*."

"Yeap, about right." He stared at Mason. "What'd'ya think we oughta do?"

It took a moment, a long set of breaths where Slate came close to losing hope, but then it happened. Like it always did. Slate watched as Mason's chin tipped up, lifting as his lips spread in a slow, satisfied smile.

"Fuck yeah. What you got, boss?"

Our History

Jock

"I cannot turn this down."

He'd known it was coming, had carried the weight in his chest all day, but hearing the words in her voice set the cement curing, dragging at him as it grew heavier and heavier.

"You're not a fool, Silly." He reached for her hand, lifted her knuckles to his lips. She rolled her fingers to clasp his, and he felt them tremble. "Too smart to work for someone else all your life, and this? Baby, this is custom-made for you. It's an opportunity of a lifetime." He'd practiced the words in his head, pleased they sounded more sincere aloud. He meant everything he said. It was all true. It just fucking sucked. "You're right. You can't turn it down."

"What does this mean for us?" Her fingers spasmed in his as she posed an impossible question. Impossible for all the reasons he'd already sorted out in his head.

If she took the offer, they'd be ending. He wouldn't make her try to keep things together, not starting out in a new city on top of taking on a challenge like stepping into a store that was bound to have drama, just because the previous manager and star artist was more than high maintenance. No, she'd have her hands full, and trekking her ass up to be with him would wear on her quickly. His job was here, his brothers and club, so he wasn't in any better position to haul himself to see her more than once a month, if that. Better to let her go gracefully, with no anger. He'd passed hour after hour coaching himself to accept the inevitable.

It still sucked.

"I hope I'll be a sweet memory for you." He lifted his gaze to her face just in time to see the devastation settle in, hope falling away and grief taking hold. Reaching deep inside himself, determined not to layer his pain on top of hers, he kept his voice steady. "And until you have to go, I'm with you. Anything you want,

Silly. I'll be here. I'll be in Chicago, if you can make time for me." Her eyes closed slowly, but not before he saw the wet swimming there. "Baby." He settled her into his lap, holding her close. "We'll take it a day at a time, yeah?"

Wordlessly, she toyed along his arms, palms smoothing up and up until she reached his neck. Then, as she always did, Silly started her exploration of him, beginning with the scars that dimpled his neck and shoulders, souvenirs from the day he should have died. Twenty-two men had rolled out on patrol that day, and scarred as he was inside and out, he was the only one still breathing.

"You got these in the war?" Silly reached out to him, then jolted and ducked her head, the movement redirected until her fingers tucked into the back pockets of her jeans, dermal implants flashing in the neon lights. Arms to the side, she swung her hips and poked him with an elbow. "I'm sorry."

"No sorries," he told her, not knowing that would be the first of a hundred such demands and reassurances between them. They'd left the club's party at Gunny's place behind and continued their night at a mutually agreed-upon bar. He hadn't done this in a long time, the flirting, and maybe never with someone like her. This woman was out of his league. Still, he wanted to reach for it. The problem was every movement, every word carried an awkwardness he

knew she could read like a book. "They're just scars." He shrugged, not sure what else to say. The scars were a permanent part of him. "If they bother you—"

"No." She angled towards him, again caught herself and halted, then lowered her voice so he had to lean in to hear her. "No, your scars don't bother me. Skin, it's meant to hold our history."

"What do you mean?" From this close he could smell her scent, an intricate musky perfume. She was sweet and gorgeous. Silly was so beautiful he'd almost been afraid it was a joke when she'd approached him back at Gunny's place. Now she was proving herself intelligent, too. A trifecta of everything he wanted. "A history how?"

"I tattoo. I am an artist." He nodded, having gotten that from their earlier introductions. "Not just the kind of flash framed on the shop walls. My favorite part is when I ink memories into people's skin, write stories into the canvas behind which they will spend the rest of their lives. A mask for some, but for others, it can be a gift of thoughtful histories they want to share with the world, or keep secret in some cases. A whispered reminder instead of a defiant shout." She shrugged, the movement graceful like a dancer. She was lean, petite. Tiny and vulnerable in a way that made him want to protect her. Even situated as he was, deliberately slouched low on a barstool in a corner, he towered over her. "Of course, some scarring can be *intentional, but most is evidence of life's interruptions. A history just the same, but one of surprise and pain instead of anticipation and pleasure." She rolled her neck, arching the delicate column, and he saw a white line transecting her skin. "My cousin wanted to learn to sword fight. I learned a lesson that day that I think of every time I see the scar. That's one of dozens." She nodded towards him. "You gained your scars in a day, yes?" He didn't respond, just held her gaze. "My lessons took decades. Our histories are different, but in some ways...the same."*

"Huh." Moved by her insight, Jock self-consciously ran a finger around the neck of his shirt. "I hadn't thought of it that way. I just always... I don't know. Ugly is all that comes to mind when I take the time to look at them." He forced a laugh that felt too loud and lasted just a beat too long, more awkwardness come home to roost. "I don't often take a mind to look at them. I try to ignore them mostly."

"I do a lot of survivor tattooing. Cancer, injury. I tattooed a toenail complete with polish on a woman last week." She smiled, still seeming as comfortable and easy with him as she'd been all night.

"A toenail? With a manicure?" Taking a chance, Jock slipped his fingers around her wrist to tug one hand out of its hiding place. He pretended to examine her fingers but knew she saw through his ruse when she tapped his nose. He'd wanted to touch her and

had read her movements earlier as a reflection of the same. It seemed he hadn't been wrong.

"Yes, complete with a pedicure." She teasingly emphasized the word. "She'd had an accident as a child and lost the first joint off her index toe. When she called me for a consult, she said it always made her ill at ease. She'd paint her toenails, make her feet pretty, but then hide them away. The first day she wore sandals was walking away from my chair." Silly pressed her palm to his as if measuring and smiled up at him when her fingers barely reached to the middle of his. "That felt good."

He spread his fingers and let her thread their hands together, working at it until he could hold her hand, clasped palm to palm. "I bet it did. That's important, then, what you do."

"I've done intricate breast pieces and shields to disguise or augment mastectomy scars. Helping the women regain a sense of control is important. Those pieces aren't about decoration so much as they are a statement of power. 'This is my body. I will not cede it to cancer.' That's what I keep in my mind when I do those designs." She leaned into him, her shoulder pressed tightly to his ribs. The pressure was exquisite, and he fought to keep from going hard. "Of course"—she smiled and tilted her head, crazy-colored hair falling all around, and Jock had a vision of her in bed, spread underneath him, giving him that smile—"I also

do tattoos of butterflies and roses, often positioned at the small of a woman's back. But whatever it is, it becomes part of their history."

Jock drew in a slow, steadying breath. "I want you to be part of my history." Silly's hand stilled, and she leaned back enough to see his face, signs of her upset still present in the shining tracks of tears. "Before you go. I want you to give me that tattoo you've been drawing in your head for more than a year." She stared, eyes wide. "You think I don't know you, Sylvia? Know what you're thinking? You want to put you on me." He cradled the curve of her skull, urging her to resume her previous position. *Sometimes it's easier if I can't see.* Cheek back against his chest, she settled her hands on top of his, those clever fingers walking across each tendon and vein, mapping out the dimensions. "I want that, too."

***

Silly

Jock's words had burned, scoring a wound through her chest and into her heart, molten pain in its path.

"I hope I'll be a sweet memory for you."

She hadn't answered him, couldn't and stay whole, or at least as whole as she'd be at the end of this. He'd come to the same conclusion she had, clearly, and she hated how sweet he was being. It wasn't as if Jock wasn't feeling the same pain, because she read it on his expression every time he looked at her. Bald need and anguish, and he'd fight it, shutting it down a little at a time until all that was left was the pride in her accomplishments, his pleasure at what this would mean for her career, for her.

Selfless. When she was anything but, her brain working out scenarios where he uprooted himself and went with her, or refused to let her go with a demand she stay for him.

I would, if he asked. And he knew it, too, which was why he never would ask.

Selfless.

So the one thing he had asked, she'd give him. Somehow, she'd manufacture time to draw the things she saw in her mind. On his chest, she'd paint him with a chopper, the kind he built in the club's shop, giving it a David Mann feel without stealing any of that master's thunder. She'd put him on the back of the bike, and up until now, she'd always imagined giving herself space behind him, legs cocked up at his hips, short shorts exposing all kinds of flesh in a risqué, shop-calendar way. For his back, with the scarring, she'd have to take care and do short sessions to limit the amount of additional scarring. But she imagined a landscape with all the things important to him. Semper Fi, the American flag, a dark horizon with silhouettes of soldiers, the Marine insignia and birthday, maybe a small patch reserved for her. One of them would be a challenge, but to plan both? *I can do it.*

And even if she didn't get it all on him before she left, it would be a reason for him to visit. Even if adding to the tattoo became the sole reason he came to see her, she'd take it without question. Take it and squeeze every second out of it, give him what he'd asked for and take what she needed.

"Baby?" Jock's voice startled her, drawn out of the air just over her head. She was nestled in front of him, small spoon style, and he'd wrapped as much of himself around her as he possibly could. With his even breaths, she hadn't realized he was still awake, thinking him asleep hours ago, but his voice didn't give away he'd been sleeping, and the pain just underneath the surface said he'd been lying awake, just like her.

"Yeah?" Her voice was scarcely a whisper, but she knew he'd heard her because his arms tightened around her.

Nothing more, just an assurance they were connecting even with this.

She wanted to scream, rail at the fates who'd thrown this boulder in their path, destroying the beauty they'd been building together. She'd escaped an oppressive family, fleeing the village where she'd been born and coming to the US in the back of a covered truck. About ten years ago, Mason had found out about her status and set about making it so she never had to worry. That was after her family had followed her, when she'd found the depths of evil they were capable of. There'd been so many bodies that day, and one of them had looked just like her. A cousin who'd hooked her star to the wrong man and been driven into acts Sylvia still couldn't believe had planned to kill and impersonate her to get close to Mason and his men. *I survived*.

That was it, though. The sum total of these past years. Survival. Fear had ruled her for a long time, and it was only recently that she'd started moving past it and into something better. No longer just surviving, she was living, sucking life dry and asking for more. Silly brushed her cheek along Jock's bicep, his arm bent double under her, hand clutched between hers as she held it to her chest.

"Baby," Jock murmured again. "You okay?"

No, I'm not okay. How could I be okay, when I'm going to begin the process of tearing myself away from the only thing that's made sense in forever? She swallowed those words, feeling the burn of tears at the back of her throat. "Yeah, Jock. I'm okay."

She made and dismissed a thousand plans over the next few hours.

When sunrise came, teasing into the room with glowing streams of light, she still hadn't found any good solutions.

***

Mason

"I understand you're sending our girl down to the Big Easy."

Mason waited through the heavy sigh, then a humming false start, until Ernie finally got down to it.

"It's the right move for her. I need her. Best of both worlds, Mason my friend." More humming, then, "She's hesitant, and I understand."

"Do you, motherfucker? Do you really?" He would much rather have done this in person, but his daughter had a virus and he wanted to be close with his baby girl feeling sick. Mason shook his head. "It's the best thing for you, maybe. You get a good business salvaged by a gal you already know is loyal down to the bone. But did you think what it means for her, old man?"

"She didn't say no."

"Of course she didn't say no. Goddammit, of course she didn't. She dotes on your ass. If you asked her to go to Iowa to pick up some goddamned turkey or St. Louis for ribs, she'd be in the wind an instant later. Dotes on your ass, and you're sending her a thousand goddamned miles away? Fuck, man." He tipped his head back and stared at the wall of pictures Willa had put up in his office. The rest of the house was all about peace and harmony, at least whatever that looked like in her kooky, crazy head, but in here she'd given him biker goodness. Pictures of him and his brothers, him at rallies and parties, him rolling out in the lead on a memorial ride. She'd found pictures of his first bike and somehow managed to make it look so good that he'd kill to have that damned Indian back. That was why he didn't make business calls from in here that often. He'd get so mellow looking at the images of his life mapped out to muse over, he couldn't work up a decent rant. Tipping forwards, he planted an elbow on the desk, phone held to his bowed head. "You're giving her everything at the same time you're takin' it all away."

"She's young."

"You know when you met Sheila that she was the one?" Mason shot back without pausing, because he already knew the answer. "You see that woman in a crowd on the train platform and set out to make her yours?"

"You know I did."

"It matter how young or old you were?" He pressed his thumb against his brow, pushing hard. "It matter she was way the fuck outta your league?"

"No, it didn't. I saw her, and I would have followed her to the ends of the earth."

"But you didn't have to. You saw her, followed her home like a goddamned stalker, and then set about makin' her yours. But she lived here, you lived here. She worked here, and so did you. All the hard stuff was taken care of. You didn't have to bend over backwards to make time for her, didn't have to align time zones or any shit like that." He scoffed, hoping to drive home his point. "Sheila made it easy on you, wrapping her life up in yours without any argument, because she saw that, too."

"Yes, but still there were things to work out. It wasn't all buttons and balloons, *jefe*."

"Silly trots her happy ass to Fort Wayne a minimum five hours one way, doin' that every other weekend. Ten hours round trip, if the traffic gods are shining on her. She organizes her schedule to give herself those days, even though she could make a lot of fuckin' flash if she worked Friday nights and Saturdays. She's done that without complaining, done it in a way that you and the shop get what you need of her, meanin' time standin' at her chair with someone's ass in it, and she can still give herself to her man in the way he needs her, too." Mason paused a beat, but Ernie didn't have anything to say. "Her man, he does the same. No discussion, no askin' permission, just movin' things around so he can give his girl what she needs from him. Time, and time, and time. That's all they ask of the other. He trots his happy ass to Chicago at least once a month, doin' that when he only gets bits of her time, but they're all the more precious for that. And you're moving her to New Orleans and fuckin' that up for the both of them." He made an angry sound far back in his throat. "Because you need her so you can keep a shop open. You're willing to ask her to throw away what she's got here, because she dotes on you and you asked, and she'll do it. She'd open a vein and bleed for you, you asked it. So she'll do it. She'll go. It'll kill her, probably. Definitely kill her man. Inconvenience you short term because you'll have to run your goddamned shop by yourself up there, but what's that matter? You'll have gotten what you need, right? Fuck, Ernie. I used to like you."

He disconnected, not giving his old friend time to respond, too angry to handle any more self-serving excuses.

"Gonna have to find a way."

He looked up at the wall of images, gaze tracking from frame to frame, taking in the faces, places, the essence of brotherhood that seeped from all of them.

"Got to find a way."

One Day

Jock

"Fuck." He slung the wrench into the toolbox and stalked to the sink to run cool water over his bleeding knuckles, the water slowly turning from red to pink, then back to clear.

"Need stitches?" Gunny's question drifted over from where he sat next to his own bike.

At least the man hadn't felt the need to jump up and mother Jock. Sharon's pregnancy had him acting like a hen, fluffing his feathers around his chicks to keep them safe, those chicks not just his kids, but his brothers, too. Last night Jock had caught him opening beers for a group standing at the bar in the clubhouse, saving their fingers from the roughened edges of the lids.

"Nah, I'll just wrap it up. It'll be fine." He scoffed. "What's one more scar." Water off, he dabbed at the rough-edged wound with his greasy rag. White flashed deep inside, and he winced. "Well, maybe."

Without standing, Gunny bellowed, *"Red,"* over his shoulder towards the office.

A moment later, the door clicked open and Jock heard, "Jesus fucking Christ on a goddamned stick. What the fuck you need, Gunny?"

"Jock needs stitches." Gunny waved his hands over his head. "I'm greasy."

"And I'm busy," Red retorted.

Jesus, they're worse than ever. "Fuck you, assholes. I can take myself to see the doc." He flipped them both off, grimacing as the movement set up a pounding throb in his finger. "Dammit."

"I will take him." Soft, sultry and slow, Silly's voice washed over him, bringing such a sublime sense of relief it first stroked over him like velvet, then struck deep with pain that had nothing to do with his finger.

She'd been due in yesterday but texted late in the day that she had to stay the night in Chicago. Her message had been detailed and explained all the reasons why, but all he'd been able to focus on was the sinking feeling that she was beginning to pull away.

Silly had accepted Ernesto's offer, of course. She'd said there'd been lots of intense discussion around his vision, ensuring hers would line up, and then it was done. Paperwork filed to get her licensing secured in Louisiana, paperwork to get her on the books as a manager, paperwork to break her lease. Jock had gone to her as often as she'd allow, but she hadn't been lying—it was busy and time-consuming.

The takeover date was set for two weeks from yesterday. He planned to drive down with her, not liking the idea of Silly taking that trip on her own, which she'd found hilariously sweet, if the amount of time her mouth had been on him was anything to measure. They'd have the trip down, and he was planning on stretching their journey out for three days, maybe four. He'd be in her new space with her for a week, helping with the move-in and settling, taking evenings to explore her new neighborhood.

Then he'd leave her behind, climb on a bike he was bringing back for a brother, and watch her dwindle to a speck in his rearview.

So now, he took a moment to absorb that soft and pain that came from hearing her voice, and when he turned, he did it with a practiced smile at the ready, beating back the hopelessness that seemed closer every day. "Hey."

"Hey yourself." She reached past him to the work surface and yanked a handful of paper towels off the roll, then plucked the greasy rag out of his fingers, grimacing. "Don't you know anything about rudimentary first aid? The last thing you do is introduce more chance of infection to an open wound." Shaking her head, she cradled his hand on the nest of white paper, bending her head to look at the injury. "He'll live," she announced flatly, and Gunny chuckled.

"Gimme," Jock whispered, because the moment she'd gotten up in his space, the scent of her had hit him, that damned spicy musk she favored, because his girl was anything but vanilla. Just the smell of her made his mouth water, and he knew she saw his checked desire when her breath caught on a gasp. He urged her, "Kiss me, baby."

Silly rolled up to her toes, and he bent deep so their mouths met in a slow slide of wet and hot. "Mmmm. I missed you." Her murmur was for his ears only, her lips still traveling along his jaw. "Let's get this seen to, and you can take me home."

What he'd called home for nearly as long as he'd been in Fort Wayne was a bedroom in Domino's house. He and his brother had made it work, even after Silly inserted herself into his life, but at times, privacy was hard to come by there. This weekend was one of those times, as Domino's extended family was in town and no fewer than seven nieces and nephews had declared their uncle's house prime sleepover territory.

"Better idea," he muttered, nuzzling into the bend of her neck. "Got us a suite for the weekend." He hadn't stayed there last night, no matter it'd been paid for. When she'd had to cancel at the last minute, Jock had ensured his dog would be cared for, thrown a leg over his bike, and ridden through the moonlight to a lake over in Ohio. Gunny had a cabin Jock had been to a couple of times, and he'd gone there and planted his ass in Sharon's porch swing, then watched the ripples in the water glint and shine as wind danced across the surface of the lake. He'd stayed there until time to come into the garage, that frustration and exhaustion probably part cause of his carelessness with the torque wrench. "My bag's already there. Gimme a minute and I'll pull the bike in, leave it locked up in here for the weekend."

"Will you be able to ride with stitches in that finger?" Silly pulled back and stared up at him, her fingers still cupped around his hand. He nodded, not sure where she was going with this. Quiet but no less intense for that, she said, "Then we'll come back here after the hospital, leave my car, and I'll ride with you."

She was no stranger to his bike. From the first night she'd spent in his bed, every time they were together, weather permitting—which in Indiana was chancy eight months out of the year—they'd take at least one ride, her wrapped around him in a way he was more than fond of. He knew she enjoyed it, not to the extent he did, where it'd become necessary for his sanity, but she'd made it clear she liked snuggling up against his back, tits pressed tight, hands roaming as she wished as long as she didn't distract too much.

Before the move had surfaced on the horizon, he'd been pacing himself, wanting to take her temperature before he asked her to wear a vest for him. His close brothers had razzed him, told him she needed a Property Of patch, and he'd come around to their way of thinking. Then things changed.

"Okay, Silly." If she needed a ride on his bike this weekend to clear her head, or just because, a half a dozen stitches in his finger wouldn't stop him from giving that to her.

***

Silly

She glanced over to where Jock leaned against the inside of the passenger door of her car. Eyes closed, head back, he looked like he could be sleeping, if she ignored the lines of tension in his face.

"Hurting much?" She kept her voice level, quiet in case he was asleep, even if she didn't think it possible. He'd sliced the hell out of his finger, deep into the muscles just above the knuckle and down over the bend. The paper towels she'd wrapped around it were soaking through, pink, red, and maroon slowly discoloring the surface.

"Not too." His voice wasn't clipped, but the strain was obvious to her. "I didn't expect you for a couple of hours."

"I was training one of the other artists how to order supplies and other things. Turned out she's used the software before, so it went fast." She slowed and stopped at a red light. "I didn't find you at Domino's, so I took a chance you were at the garage."

"Looking for me, huh?" Glancing at him, she saw his expression had shifted into a smile, the barest curve of his lips, but it was real. More real than the fake one he'd turned on her back at the garage, and she reached over to trail her fingers down his thigh. "For you, Silly, I'll always make myself easy to find."

"Obliged." Her wry, single-word response drew a chuckle from him, and she focused on traffic until they were pulling into the hospital. "I'll drop you at the ER." She twisted the wheel, startled when his injured hand landed on her thigh.

He pressed it deep, and she glanced to see him shaking his head. "Just park. It's my finger, not my legs." She rolled her eyes but did as directed, not surprised when he was out of the car before her. Silly fell into step beside him, amused as ever that he slowed his paces to match her shorter legs. *Just one more way he shows how he cares.* They angled across the parking lot towards the broad sliding doors. He muttered under his breath, his voice more a growl than anything, "Fuckin' hate hospitals."

"I didn't know that."

"Spend enough time in a place where they goddamned well torture you and see how you like it." She stepped up onto the sidewalk and stopped, turning back to see he was frozen at the curb. "The smell's the worst. Fuckin' worst, and I hate it all, but that's the worst. Puke and piss, bleach, and so much goddamned despair, you could milk it and make a meal out of the pain." His tone was flat, and his eyes were unfocused, dim in a way she recognized. "Don't matter where I am, I smell it and I know what's in store for me."

"Not today." She took a step towards him and leaned in, palm to his chest. "Not today, Jock. I promise you, I'll make sure you only have sweet things to smell, and I can't take the pain, but I can make sure you don't fall into it. If that's what you're worried about." The way his heart thundered underneath her touch said she had it right. "Not today. And if you want to go, I'll hit up a pharmacy and get what I need to sort you out. I'd like to know for certain you didn't fuck up a tendon or something, because that'd impact how you earn your living. You need your hands, just like I need mine." She looped an arm around his neck, pulling him near. "But if you want to go, we'll go, no questions asked."

His gaze flicked from the building behind her to her face, then back, still distant. They stood like that for a minute, two, three. He took a deep breath and bent his neck, burrowing deep, lips to her skin. Soft fluttering, then the gentle wet glide of his tongue, and she wrapped both arms around his shoulders as his good hand slid up her back, fingers buried in her hair.

"I'm good." Said against her throat, the quiet words still made her shiver, the brush of his mouth pleasure and pain. Pleasure because she loved it, loved having him touch her like that, and pain because their time was running out, the looming move casting its thick, suffocating shadow on everything they did together. "I'm good, Silly. You make me that way."

"No, Jock. You do the work, you get the praise. You're making yourself better, every day." Silly twisted her neck and rolled to her toes, steadying herself on his shoulders. Mouth to the hinge of his jaw, just by his ear, she whispered, "And watching you put in that work, seeing the shine in your eyes as you take back everything you need to be you, makes me so glad to know you. Just to experience, even at a remove, the beauty of you taking back the promise you hold inside, I'm proud to be right here with you."

He made a choked sound and his arm tightened around her. They stood there for a long time, a quiet oasis of stillness on a busy sidewalk, in front of a busy hospital, and Silly knew walking through those doors would break this moment, so she held on just as tight, needing this with him.

"I'm ready," he murmured. He gave her a squeeze and she returned it, settling back on her heels as she studied his face. His eyes had lost that glazed look, were alert, and he stared at her in a way she knew he was taking her in. She nodded, stepped to the side, and curled her hand around his good one, letting him lead the way.

***

Slate

"Where's Jock?" He looked around the garage, scanning every visible face. "Gunny, man, where's he at? I got something for him."

Gunny grunted from where he stood in front of the low sink, then glanced at Slate over his shoulder. "Silly showed, took him in to get his hand looked at. Man fucked it up." He tipped his chin towards Jock's work station, the bay tidy, but a splattering of dark red beside the bike lift. "Fucked it *up*. What do you need?"

"I talked to a friend, found out a little bit about that neighborhood Silly's movin' to in Louisiana." He stopped talking when Gunny straightened, then grabbed a rag and turned around slowly. "Wanted to go over a couple of things with him. She's down, means she's down for the weekend. I'll catch him Monday."

"What'd you find out?" Gunny's jaw jutted out, and his lips were thin, pressed tightly together. "Anything wrong with where she's gonna lay her head, brother?"

"Couple of interesting things, is all. Nothin' bad, brother. We wouldn't let Silly get stuck in a place that wasn't safe. Not even temporarily." He looked at Gunny for a long minute, considered his next question, considered it again, and still asked it. "If Sharon wasn't happy being away from Vanna, wanted to move down, or if Kitt needed her to be there and not here, what would you do?"

Gunny's immediate answer was "Give my woman what she needed." No hesitation, no question in his mind, just straight-from-his-gut honesty. "However that happened, she'd be happy. She ate shit for too goddamned long for me to give her a moment where she's not happy. I'd give her whatever the fuck she needed, man. Just like you would Ruby."

Slate nodded slowly, deliberating his next question. From the determined jut of Gunny's jaw, he decided the man would be more pissed if he didn't ask. "You think we're going to lose Jock?"

"Can't lose the brotherhood forged in fire." Slate sighed, but Gunny wasn't done. "Don't matter where he hangs his hat, he'll always be my brother."

"You think he knows that?" Gunny's head shake was as slow as Slate's nod had been. "Yeah, me either. You think we can convince him before they take that road trip?" That earned him a quiet blink, then a brief shake. "Yeah, me either."

***

Jock

"Jesus." He stared at his hand in disbelief. "Doc, you know I ain't gonna leave that shit there, right?"

His middle finger was cocooned in a mix of gauze, cotton, and tape so wide it forced his other fingers down and away, leaving him flying a big white bird all the time.

Muffled laughter made him glance towards where Silly perched on the foot of his bed. Close enough if he leaned forwards, he could catch a hint of her scent, but far enough away to show her belief in his strength, even if it didn't feel like he'd been strong today. Shoes abandoned, she'd folded her legs under herself, graceful as ever, and watched the process of him getting his ass first reamed out by a doc who happened to be more than friends with the club, then cleaned up, stitched up, and now wrapped up. Stitching he could handle, short, sharp flashes of pain followed by a slow dragging burn as the fibers slid through his flesh, but—as a complete surprise—the cleaning process that came before hadn't been at all comfortable, especially when he wouldn't let them deaden the wound before working on it. It wasn't about being macho, but if they'd done a nerve block at the elbow like they'd talked about, his arm would have been in a sling for hours, and not able to give Silly that ride.

So Jock had gritted his teeth, let Silly hold his other hand, and talked about inconsequential things while someone pressed a blistering hot poker of fire deep into his finger. The one time he'd glanced over, it didn't make sense, because the pretty little nurse had his finger angled over a pan and was aiming a gentle stream of water at the gash. Then she'd picked up tweezers and he'd flicked his gaze back up at Silly.

Now he was stitched—twenty-two of the damned things, which he'd felt was overly enthusiastic—and bandaged, extravagantly so, and ready to go. *About fucking time.*

"Don't tear out my handiwork." The doc flashed a smile at him, his Aussie-tinted accent still sounding strange to Jock's ears. "You'll be right as rain in a couple of weeks. Just go easy on anything too strenuous, yeah?"

"God save me from medics. I'll go easy, Bulldog." Jock gave the man a crooked smile to cut any sting from his words. Bulldog was a friend and had been a rock for Jock since Gunny introduced them. "Thanks, brother."

"Yeah, yeah." Headed towards the curtain, the doc lifted a hand and waved over his shoulder, folding the rest of his fingers at the last moment, middle digit standing proud. *What an asshole.* "Be well, brother."

"I like him," Silly said with no preamble, swung her legs off the edge of the bed, and jumped down with a little hop. She shuffled into her shoes, head dipped to look down. Jock already had one foot on the floor, so he caught her by surprise as he tugged her close. He twisted, planting the other foot so she was sandwiched between his legs. "He's no-nonsense. Just straight to the point and taking care of business. I can see why your brothers like him."

"You know Gypsy?" She should, the man had started his life with the RWMC in Chicago, so it was no surprise she smiled along with her nod. "Bulldog is his woman's brother. What are the fuckin' chances of that?"

"Kelsey?" Palm flat against the wall of his chest, she patted him gently. "I like her. That's good. Good for her and Gypsy. He's one of the good ones, you know?" She paused, hummed, and patted him again, soft and slow, her hand gliding along his sternum, almost like she was settling herself with touching him. "I'm glad she's got family close. It's hard enough starting over, but doing it without knowing anyone would be worse." *Fuck*. She'd just described her next few months. "Now…" She lifted his hand, laughing aloud at the absurdity of the bandaging in place on his finger. "Let me unravel this puzzle and make something more manageable of it."

He gave her silence, patiently let her study the tape and gauze before she began to peel back the many layers. Watching her face, he saw the moment the intensity hit, giving her expression a feral cast, the same she wore when running her tattoo gun. So he gave her another few seconds, letting her drill deep into that zone she hit in her head when she was concentrating. Then he asked, "You happy, Silly?"

"Of course." Head tipped to one side, she angled her eyes up to catch his, then smiled softly as she looked back down. "I've a handsome man in front of me who I care for a great deal, and he's letting me care for him. How could I not be happy?"

"You're gonna be happy again, right?"

"Jock, I'm always happy. I'm Silly." She had the finger stripped down to the basics, fibrous strands of tape crisscrossed over the stitches. Leaning towards the cart where she'd laid the rest, she plucked out a few small pieces of whatever she deemed acceptable, then concentrated on his finger again. "You make me happy."

And that right there was why he should have broken off with her weeks and weeks ago when she'd told him about the job.

Jock grunted, throat tight. He forced out on a thick whisper a fact he knew well. "I'm a selfish asshole." Her eyes darted up, gaze locking with his. "But I can't see my way to give up even one of these last days with you. I'll make you happy, Sylvia. My hand to God, I'm going to make you happy, and I'll make sure you're in a place to stay that way once you're in New Orleans. Swear to God."

"Jock." She stood straight, even then having to tip her chin up to look him in the face. "Baby, I didn't mean to make you mad."

"Oh, I'm not mad, sweetheart." *Lie*. Furious at himself and life, for giving him all of this, all of her— just to take it away again. "Just sayin' how it's gonna be. You with me?"

"Jake."

He pressed, leaning into her as he reached his good hand to cup the back of her head. "You with me, Sylvia? I'm going to be that sweet memory, and I'm going to do my damnedest to keep making you smile and keep making you happy, long as I can. So now, are you with me?"

"Yes, Jake." The smile that curled her lips told him her words were a lie, too. Sad and small, it didn't belong to the woman he knew. A woman who'd taken one look at a man across a room and set about to make him hers. "I'm with you."

"Damn straight you are." He jerked his chin at his finger, which now looked more like a finger and less like a failed attempt at a balloon animal. "You done?"

She studied his finger, watching him test the curl and reach allowed by the swelling, stitches, and light bandages, and nodded.

"Let's go ride."

They did, her hair loose in the wind, not caring what kind of tangles it bought her at the end of it. He aimed the bike back to the remote lake where he'd been the night before. Slowing, he smiled at how she clutched him when he cautioned her to be still as he turned onto the narrow, potholed dirt drive. Riding the ridge between the ruts, the headlight carved a path through the dark and trees, folding the noise of the bike back around them until it felt like his skin was vibrating. There was a curve at the end, and once he rounded that, her hands clutched again, this not out of fear but a reaction to the beauty spread out before them.

The moon had risen, bright and well on its way to full, only a tiny crescent carved from one edge. The wind was low and slow, but it rippled the surface of the water enough to capture that light and cast it back a thousand different sparkling ways.

Jock rolled onto the concrete pad beside the cabin, heeled the kickstand down as he killed the engine. Silence rushed in where only noise existed a moment before, just in time for that to be broken by her reverent whisper, the one word singing out long and low. *"Baby."* He heard the inrush of air as she sucked in a breath, only to push out a fraction of it on another whisper. "Jake, this is so beautiful."

"No, Silly." He leaned against her and turned his head to see she was looking at him. "You're beautiful. This is God's grace at work."

Jock found the porch swing was far more appealing when shared with Silly. Boots and shoes lying in a tangle on the wood of the porch, the seat of the swing still warm from the day's sun, he rested sideways, knees bent while Silly reclined against his chest. She turned partly, and he caught her before she could slip, her so enthralled by the moon on the water or the stars beyond that she didn't seem to notice. Or she trusted him to keep her safe. Which he'd do, always.

"Gunny owns this?" Soft and sweet, she cuddled closer as night drew down the dew, chilling the air. "You come here often?"

"Not often, no. And it's worth sayin', never when he's here just him and Shar." He chuckled. "When he brings the kids, makes it a family event, that's another matter. Tank likes the water and his pups, and loves his kids and Shar. My Tankster would stand between those kids and a hurricane if he had to."

"Tank." She snorted, then said fondly, "His name so suits him."

"That it does."

"What will you do with him when you help me move?" Jock swallowed at the change in her tone, gone from warm and sweet to flat and sad in a moment. "You won't have to board him, will you?"

"Nah, Gunny's already said he'd be happy to keep him as long as I need." Jock stroked up her side, tangling his fingers in her hair. "Cade is pleased that her Tank is gonna be there for a good, long visit."

"She's a cutie."

"That she is." He teased a knot out, then gently searched until he found another and started to work on that one. "You need a bandana when we head out, grab one out of my sidebag, yeah?"

"Yeah." Silly shifted. "Am I crushing you?"

"Nah, woman. You're light as a feather." She laughed, and he watched her face, needing to see that joy. "Long as you don't crush anything vital, you can stay like this long as you want."

"Wouldn't want to do that." Some of the happy left her expression. He'd opened his mouth to ask why when she added, "You might want your own Cade one day."

Her way of moving on. He tried to remind himself she wasn't being flip, or easy, because nothing in the entire process had been an easy decision. It'd been hard, much as it should have been. This was Silly's way of creating distance, building a future in her mind where Jock would be happy, have kids, find love. So, even if it killed him to do it, he'd give that to her.

"Yeah." Jock looked out at the lake, soft sounds of waves lapping on the shore the only sounds for a few minutes. "One day."

***

Silly

She stared at the scattering of boxes that lined the walls, stacked in little piles. Her art room had produced the highest number of packed and taped boxes, and she'd been meticulous about how things were stored and labeled. Silly had moved more than once and knew this end was actually the easiest part, so she'd do what was needed to make the other half easier. A portion of the boxes would be going into a storage unit in Louisiana, and the remainder to the small apartment she'd rented there. The whole of her things was enough to fill a medium-sized moving truck, currently sitting at the curb outside, ready to begin the southwards trek. They'd begin in Fort Wayne, with Mason and the other boys tomorrow, and then her time spent in the north would be over, a new chapter in her life in Louisiana awaiting. *I should be more excited.*

Noise from the other room pulled her attention, and she glanced over her shoulder.

Jock was striding through the room with an even pace, the footboard of her bed balanced in his arms. Without being asked, he'd put himself in charge of the move, organizing the truck, getting a half dozen Rebel members from the Chicago chapter to come help with the heavy items. He'd forced her to take breaks, even when she didn't want to, becoming bossy in a way she didn't recognize, but liked. He'd ordered various RWMC prospects to make fast food runs, to make trips to the store when she ran out of labels, and to the bar just down the street to buy a couple of backdoor six-packs.

True to his word, anything he could do to make it easier, he had.

That didn't mean it was easy.

Since that night they'd spent on the lakeshore, talking through to the morning so she had the vision of the sun kissing rippling wavelets in her memories, he'd been everywhere she looked. Talking to Ernie, talking to Mason and Gunny, talking to anyone he could in order to take a burden off her shoulders.

Silly drifted through the emptying rooms, mentally cataloging the few things left to manage, and realized they'd be done in another forty-five minutes, tops. She stood still for a moment, then dug her phone out and made a call of her own to set in motion what she'd planned for the rest of their evening.

It'd be another opportunity to create a shared memory, something to hold tight to after this move was done. Sifting through the moments she and Jock had shared over the past few weeks, her traitorous brain latched onto one that was beautiful but made her ache inside.

Silly knew she was asking for pain, but this was what they'd always done, talked and sorted through what everything meant to the other, until there could be a balance in how they looked at things. "How many kids you want?"

The way he stilled underneath her, she knew he didn't want to answer. He'd been gently deflecting her comments or questions that spoke to a future where they weren't together, but it was time to move past that into what they could still have between them with a thousand miles to cross. Friends, she hoped and prayed, but honestly, she'd take anything he gave her.

She felt his stillness go to rigidity as she confessed, "I've always wanted a big family. Only child here, as you know, and my playmates and friends were my cousins growing up. The ones who haven't messed up in big ways have moved on and found their own families, building lives independent of what we knew. Right now, it's just me, but I don't want that forever." She sucked in a breath. "Even with economy and costs to consider, I'd still want at least two."

"Two would be a blessing." His voice was torn and ragged, breaking apart in the nighttime air, and she heard and felt his pulse begin to race. "Two would be God's finger in my life, giving me beauty."

"True words." Smoothing his shirt with her hand, she played with the buttons on the front. "Boys or girls?"

"One of each," he told her, the torn and ragged voice no easier to listen to. With the painful words came a touch at her temple, his fingers gliding along her hairline. "Boy and a girl, best of both worlds."

"Same." The ever-present knot in her throat swelled so she could scarcely get the words out. "Pass along my love of all things beautiful to both of them. Give them room to explore what makes them happy, and help guide them to keeping it."

"Give my boy the knowledge of how to protect what matters, give my girl the lesson of knowing her worth." His fingers slid into her hair and he gripped, tipping her face up to his. "Let her know it wasn't only okay to be what she needed to be, but by giving that to the world, giving it to a man, she'd be creating her own kind of beauty." He closed the distance between them as he spoke, so he finished the final words with lips brushing against hers. "Show my boy what it means to be gifted the heart of a good woman and lend her his strength in return, give her a way to hold onto happiness."

"Jock." She'd scarcely finished the final sound before he took her mouth, gentle and searching at first, lips working against hers in a way that took her breath away with the beauty of the touch. Tongue spearing into her mouth, he took everything she offered and gave it back abundantly, taking them on a high spiral until she was panting against him.

He broke the kiss, bringing his lips to her forehead, where he pressed them for a long time, their breathing slowing, sounds of the lakeshore returning. Jock murmured, "You're going to be a brilliant mother,

Sylvia. All you have to give, the love you hold inside, you're going to be everything."

She broke free from the memory and looked to the door just as he walked through. "Jock, are you nearly finished?" Holding out a hand, she beckoned him to her, smiling when he threaded his fingers with hers.

"Yeah, baby. One last trip and I think we're golden." Three men walked in behind him, and he gestured towards the boxes wordlessly. "Landlord said to leave the keys on the kitchen counter, right?" She nodded. "Then do that, and we'll head down."

"I've got a stop I want us to make." He shrugged and smiled, happy she was giving him something else she needed. "It might take a while," she warned, and he used their joined hands to pull her closer.

"No hardship, Silly, spendin' time with you."

She rolled up high on her toes and he bent deep, giving her what she wanted—his mouth on hers, tongue slipping between her lips to stroke against hers.

"We'll see what you say in a few hours."

***

Jock

He huffed out a breath that hitched in the middle, burrowed his face into the bend of his elbow a little deeper, and schooled himself to stillness.

The leather underneath him creaked, pressure deepened on his hip, and heat flared all along his side where Silly was leaning close.

"Forty minutes more, give or take. You need a break?" Her muttered question was different from her normal speech, deeper and controlled, because Silly was in the zone. He shook his head, and she muttered, "Right then, be still." The buzz of her tattoo gun racketed loud in the room. "Another section of outlines, and we'll be done for today."

"What's the next step?" He gritted his teeth, trying to hold a groan at bay when her needle danced across his spine. "Jesus," he muttered, then swallowed hard. "Fuck, that's tender."

"Next step," she started, ignoring the other parts as just a reaction, not a request to pause, "will be to color in what I want, and shade all the rest. This is the longest session and covers a large area of skin, but once the outline's in place we'll let it heal, and then I can do the other in smaller chunks." The buzz stopped, and the burn subsided. He felt her distance herself slightly, then her forearm settled against his low back. "I didn't think you'd be down to do the full outline today, but we're nearly done. Your back is holding up really well. I'm pleased."

"You gonna show it to me?" She'd asked if he needed to see what she'd planned for the big back piece before she started or if he trusted her. Without blinking an eye, he'd stripped off his shirt and lain on the table.

"If you want." She paused and adjusted again. "When you want."

Jock didn't give a shit what it was. He knew her, and he knew it'd be stunning, no matter what it depicted. He'd watched her enough to know she always made the artwork personal to the client, and she knew him better than anyone else did. Jock figured he'd come out way ahead on this, no matter what. Her wanting to start such a big tattoo now meant they'd have to schedule significant chunks of time out into the future for her to keep working on it and eventually finish.

Speaking to that knowledge, and answering her unspoken question, he simply said, "I'm good."

I Want It

Jock

"Baby." Her whisper was guttural, hot breath gusting against his neck as she leaned her forehead into the side of his jaw. Jock was curled over her back, chest pressed tight as he could while still fucking her hard.

It was the second night on the road, and he'd stopped them early enough in Memphis to give her a private, guided tour of Graceland, since Silly was a not-so-secret Elvis fan. Two hours of his life he'd never get back, but it had made her grin bigger than he'd seen in months. She'd loved the whole experience, and once they got back to the gift shop and their guide had handed them off to the retail personnel, she'd splurged on every tchotchke the place could print a picture of the two of them on. The image had been taken with them posed in front of a backdrop that made it look like they were wandering in front of the estate gates, his arm over her shoulders and Silly cuddled into his side. He'd stopped arguing after a magnet, button, bigger button, snow globe, and coffee mug had made an appearance on the counter next to the register. Jock had let her get busy looking at shirts and bought a second set of all those to have for himself, then threw three tees for her into the bag, too. Chin tipped up, she'd grinned at him, teeth grazing across her bottom lip in a promising way.

Then he'd hauled her to a famous hotel in downtown Memphis, another surprise stop Jock had organized because the place had a flock of ducks that waddled from the lobby into the elevators and back again every day, going to and from wherever it was they lived.

Last winter he and Silly had bundled up and gone to Franke Park on a bracingly cold day and fed the ducks and geese. He'd bought grain and pellets ahead of time, because during a conversation one weekend she'd gone on and on about how angry it made her that people thought the waterfowl could live on a diet of bread. The look on her face when he'd handed her the bag of goodies for the feathered beasts had been soft and sweet, and worth stepping in any number of piles of goose shit.

Today when they'd walked into the hotel lobby, she'd seen the ducks, whirled in place, and given him that same look. Soft and sweet, and so full of love he'd wanted to ravish her right there. He'd settled for a quick brush of his mouth against hers before her whispered, "You are so getting laid tonight," had him hustling through check-in and up to the room with their bag.

"Right"—she sighed, whined softly, and kissed his neck on a plea—"there. Right...there. Please."

Jock tipped his neck, dipped his head, and curled around her just a little more. Hips working fast, he was taking her hard, but the wet between her legs and the way her pussy clutched at him said she not only didn't mind, she was into it as much as he was. The seducing sound of flesh meeting flesh echoed through their room. She bowed her back, tipping her ass, and he slid deeper on a groan.

"God *damn*, Sylvia." She had one hand on the headboard, elbow locked, holding fast against his thrusts, pushing back to take him harder. "You're so fucking everything." He looped an arm around her waist, pulling her onto him, then slid his hand across her belly, slipping his fingers through her sleek wet, seeking and finding the piercing he sought. She gasped when he flicked hard, then keened, high and breathless, when he teased and twisted, pressing her hood into her clit with one fingertip. "Come all over me, baby."

With a soft, garbled cry of his name, she did.

He slowed, giving her time to take in what he'd given to her, and when her mewls had turned back to whimpers, powered up again. "So fuckin' hot, baby. Never had anything like what you give me. Never, baby." He reared up, hand on each of her hips as he guided her movements, watching her toss that hair he loved so much, colorful against the white of the hotel sheets, skin silkier than those same expensive sheets, her dark against that stark white giving him a view to brand into his brain, something to keep forever. "Never, baby. I'm there, baby."

"Go, Jake." She panted, breaths separating the words. "Go, baby. Love taking you like this. Love you."

Those words, something he'd never expected to hear from her lips, slashed deep inside him. Something he'd known from how she looked at him, from how she was with him, but hearing it—he grunted, groaned, and absorbed the shock of electricity that entered him where he was buried inside her, curled around his balls, up his spine, and exited his mouth on a growled, "I fuckin' love you, too."

She contorted her body, neck arching so she could look at him, and blinked, that damned soft look overlaying her face. "Baby."

He didn't say anything else, holding tight to her body, thumbs smoothing over the curve of her ass as his hips moved erratically, chasing the electricity again, sparkles of it flaring from his dick to the top of his head, scalp crawling with the feeling. He didn't say it, but he looked straight at her, staring hard, hoping she saw it in his face like he could hers, hoping he was an open book she wanted to read. Someone she wanted to take to bed every night, folded around her like he always did, keeping her warm, safe, and loved. So much love.

He bent, pressed his lips to her shoulder, brushing up in a caress until he had to leave her skin to capture her mouth. Tongues slipped and slid in a slow, timeless dance. She shivered under him, the chill of the air conditioning stealing heat from her sweaty body, even covered as she was by him. On a whisper he told her, "You get in the bed. I'll be back." *She's so fuckin' pretty.* He gave her a peck, then another before pulling back. "Gotta deal with the rubber." Corner of her mouth still curled in that soft smile, Silly nodded. "Back in a minute, baby." He anchored the condom on his dick as he pulled out, then curled his hand around her pussy, cupping and massaging. Stripping the condom off his cock, he asked, "You okay, Sil?"

"Yeah, Jock. I'm good." She sighed, and he gave her hips a shove, toppling her sideways in the bed. That earned him a giggle.

Jock paused in the bathroom doorway. Silly was already under the covers and smoothing them down her body, the most beautiful woman he'd ever known. She held his heart, and he knew now, he held hers.

I can't fuckin' do this.

"I'll be back." She looked up, the flash of a piercing telling him she'd cocked a brow. "I can't not, baby." Her expression sharpened as she realized he was talking about more than this moment, but she didn't respond. Didn't move. "I know I said it." He shook his head. "But I can't. I'll be back. I'll find a way to make it work." He twisted and tossed the rubber into the trash, then turned back to her. "You want it, I'll make it happen."

"Do you want that, Jock?" Her voice was strong, stronger than he'd expected. Her gaze never left him as she prompted, "Do you?"

"Fuck yeah. Thoughts of leaving you in a few days are tearing me up, Sylvia. You want it, want me? I'll figure out a way."

The silence stretched between them, the mood growing heavier with every breath. *Fuck.* He'd read her wrong. What she'd said, it was in the moment they'd been in, no more. *I can't hold her to that. Can't fault her. Won't do that to her.* What he'd said stood, and if she believed anything, he knew she'd hold those words close.

"I want it."

His breath gusted out in a rush of relief.

Her hands moved slowly, delicate fingers dancing across the linen as the covers got smoothed again. "More than I can say, Jake. It's been—" She choked on a laugh and turned her head to the side. "The best and worst weeks of my life."

Her admission only made him more determined. "I'm gonna find a way to get you only that best part from here on out, Sylvia."

Soft and plaintive, she asked, "Why are you still so far away?"

Two strides had him at the foot, one knee in the bed beside her feet, and then he was planked over her, forearms shoved into the mattress on either side.

She stared up at him, then told him again, "I love you, you know that?"

Relieved, so relieved he felt like he was flying, Jock teased her gently. "You told me once you didn't do love."

She gave him a watery smile and cupped his cheeks. "I didn't know love."

He lost himself in her kiss, let it grow between them until she was whining, teeth working at his lips.

Mouth to her ear, wrapped up in her arms, he promised, "You do now."

***

Silly

She soothed cream across Jock's back, taking care at all the places where the wounds she'd driven into his skin hadn't yet healed. He stirred restlessly, muttering, "Itches."

"It will for only a couple more days, max. It looks—" She swept her gaze from the tops of his shoulders to the curve of his ass. "Amazing. I'm very pleased."

It was time to pack their little bag and get on the road. They would arrive at the apartment by midafternoon, and then she'd be an official resident of Louisiana. As he'd promised, even this trip had been filled with beauty and happiness, with Jock surprising her every step along the way.

"You ready, baby?" He twisted away from her, rocking to one hip and pushing up on a locked arm. Reaching out, he fluffed her hair, then swept it over her shoulders and slipped the backs of his folded knuckles across her cheek. The stitches were gone, but the scar was still stark and red, raised and angry looking. He didn't care, had told her as much when she offered some scar cream, smiling at her as she fussed over him.

"Yeah. I'm set."

"Lemme grab a tee and we'll be ready to rock and roll." He exited the bed on the other side, hitched his jeans, bent to their bag and pulled out a gray T-shirt. She watched him tug it over his head, holding it out in the back so it didn't drag across his tender back. Jeans still unfastened, hanging off his hips, tee molding to his body, she stared at him as he moved to finish dressing. "What?" he asked as he put on socks, then dealt with the jeans, finally shoving his feet into his boots.

The profound feeling unspooling inside her chest couldn't be contained, and it spilled out in the form of terrifying words she didn't try to stop.

"I love you, Jake Tinney. Moon and back, you're the one for me. I hope you know that. I hope I can give that to you so you don't question it. I don't know how we're going to—" She broke off, because he was moving towards her with purpose, brows drawn down over his eyes. She picked back up, talking faster to get it out there before he shut her down. "How we're going to make this work. I don't know. But you told me you'd make it work, and I believe you. You'll tell me what you need from me, and I'll do it. Want me to turn this gig down, even now? I'd do it."

Silly said no more because he'd closed her mouth with his, arms tight around her waist and shoulders. He bent and lifted her, and she wrapped her legs around his waist as far as she could, arms around his neck. The kiss went on and on, dwindling down to sweet glides and pecks and she'd do something, make a noise, and he'd be gone again, taking her soaring right alongside him.

He broke away finally, burying his face against her neck. On a mutter, he told her what he was feeling, and it took her breath away again.

"I hated sleeping these past weeks, didn't want to miss a moment with you. Didn't matter I was gonna dream of you. Holding the real thing in my arms made more sense. Go to work sleepless, see you everywhere. That damn mug you bought me, the calendar you got me, the set of metric tools you knew I'd never buy—you're everywhere in my life, and I like it that way, baby. We get to your apartment, maybe I don't leave. Maybe I do, but it's just to take care of what I gave my word I'd do, take that bike back north. Maybe I do, and it's for a couple of weeks to settle my shit, and figure what the club's going to need from me. Doesn't matter if I leave or not, I'm still right here, and you're with me. Everywhere." His tongue trailed a hot path up her neck until he traced the curve of her ear. "I don't know what the next couple of weeks hold, but I know without a goddamned doubt that I fuckin' love you, Sylvia Perez."

It took her a moment, but once she'd gathered herself and was certain she wouldn't burst into tears on the spot, she arched up and put her mouth near his ear, and gave it back to him. "I'm on you, Jock. When you look at it, you'll see everything, including my love for you."

***

Gunny

"Man's a natural, eh." Jase lounged back, tipping his chair up on two legs. "You should see Jock at the rink with the kiddos. He's already been working on fundamental skills with four different age groups and killing it." He pumped a fist, then held it up for Gunny to give him a pound. "Killing it."

"That's good, then. Glad you talked to him about it. Got you some help finally." Gunny rose from his chair and strolled the ten feet to the grill, lifting the lid to check the progress on the chicken breasts and pork chops he was cooking. "Who's at the rink tonight, with him gone and you here?" A heavy sigh from behind him made Gunny turn to find Jase's chin tipped up, eyes on the barely visible glimmer of stars overhead. "What?"

"Jock, man, he's been through hell and back, you know?" Gunny nodded, staying quiet so Jase could get whatever was on his mind out into the air, where together they could tackle it. "Man's been through all that, you'd expect the universe to cut him some slack, eh? Bitch is shitting on him big-time."

"You mean the deal with Silly?" Jase nodded and Gunny returned his attention to the grill, using the tongs to flip over the pieces of meat. The pop and sizzle filled the silence for a moment, then he heard the sweet faraway sounds of children's laughter drifting from the house. He closed the lid and stalked back to his chair. Tank the Larger rested next to it, and the mastiff lifted his massive head as Gunny sat. He reached out and ruffled the dog's ears, selecting his words carefully. Jase was his brother-in-law as well as his brother, and he loved him, but Jase could be touchy about how entitled so much of his life had been. "Jock's a good man who's had a shit hand dealt out to him. Fate, the universe, or what-the-fuck-ever you wanna call it, doesn't give a shit about whether it's fair or not. She's not about balance, not in the short term, at least. But he deserves more. You got that right in one, brother."

"You should see him with the kids, man. He's so good. One of the good ones, eh. He'd make a hell of a dad, if he and Silly stuck it out. Maybe she won't be gone forever." Jase's voice carried a note of wistfulness, and Gunny knew his own disbelief showed in his expression when Jase's mouth twisted down. "They'd make pretty kids between them."

Gunny looked towards the house, fingers still working across Tank's head in even strokes. Sharon stood in the kitchen window, head turned to the side—and from the intent expression on her face, she was watching one of their kids doing whatever miraculous feat they'd dreamed up today. "I know it's not your thing, and that's good, because your thing isn't my thing. I'd never be able to deal with the tribe you've got roaming through your house any given day."

Jase snorted a laugh and Gunny glanced over at him, feeling a grin tipping up the corners of his mouth. Jase and his woman DeeDee had adopted an orphaned family of kids tied to the club, then fostered others as needed.

"Jock thought he had a chance at that once. You've heard about what his wife did to him?" Jase nodded. "Once a man longs to see his eyes on a child's face, nothing else measures up. He can make do, working at the rink like he is, that'd help, for sure. But deep down? I do not doubt that's his ask. And with how he loves Silly, has loved her for this long? You know he's carried that wish with him, deep inside. I don't see him giving up on that."

"I don't either, eh." Jase stretched and thumped the chair's front legs down to the ground, startling Tank into a deep, rumbling groan. "This trip is supposed to be his last goodbye, from how he described it."

Gunny grunted, folded his hands behind his head, and stared up at the stars like Jase had been a minute ago, the sky a deeper indigo already. He knew how it was to love a woman worth everything, and he couldn't imagine Jock giving it up. "I'll believe that shit when I see it."

"I already lined up another coach." Jase's statement held regret sharing space with hope. "I like Jock, and he's good with the kids. Gives me satisfaction to see him like that." He shrugged. "But DeeDee likes my ass at the table for supper."

"Now that—" Gunny chuckled and smiled when he felt the heavy weight of Tank's chin on his thigh. "That, I'll believe."

Shit Happens

Jock

He surveyed the section of neighborhood he could see from the patio of Silly's new apartment, then looked back inside at what had been a jumble of boxes just two days ago and was now at least a temporary home. She was month-to-month on the lease, giving her time and room to look for a permanent place. "Baby," he called out, grinning as she leaned around a corner from the kitchen to aim a questioning look at him. "This does not suck." She rolled her eyes and disappeared again.

They were in Hammond, not New Orleans, which was fine with both of them. The city was close enough for a night out but far enough that Hammond felt more like a small town, something he was a huge fan of.

Her new shop was fucking awesome. After some discussion, they'd made it the first stop when they hit town, and Jock had enjoyed watching his woman walk in, rubber-soled sneakers muted on the floor, voice soft as she introduced herself around, and seeing the respect, quiet but there, from every artist in that building to her.

Her skills were known, seeing as she'd been on Ernesto's show more than a dozen times in one season alone. With how she approached them, collaboratively instead of gagging for the authority granted by the position she'd be assuming, he'd watched as something more important than appreciation for her skills started to develop— admiration for her as a person. In those first few hours, she'd laid a strong foundation, then made time every day to sit down with each of the artists. All of them. The ones who'd be working for her, sure, but also the ones renting chairs, a gesture he'd seen was valued.

"Thought we'd go out tonight." He was down to only four days before he had to pick up the bike and roll north. No matter their long goals had changed, he had to stick to the short-term plan for now. There was no good solution in sight, and a telephone approach to Gunny had earned him a "fuck you" and a disconnect, which told him how his brother felt about him leaving town, and by necessity, leaving the RWMC.

"You pick a place already?" Her voice floated from the apartment and Jock smiled. This, just this, would be worth everything. Having a conversation with his woman about going out after a long day, not wanting her to cook for him, because she'd been on her feet and on her ass in a chair talking about business details, personalities, costs, and laws until she'd said her head was swimming when she got home.

"Yeah, place called Trudette's. Just up the way." He stepped through the patio doors, turned and secured the lock, then dropped the wooden dowel he'd bought and cut for the bottom track. Better than a lock. If the door couldn't slide, it couldn't be opened, period. Thieves would have to break the glass to get in. A small black box rested against the glass, a tiny green light blinking from the backside. He'd bought an impact alarm, too. So if someone broke the glass and Silly missed hearing the noise, the piercing shriek of the alarm would capture her attention and hopefully run the assholes off. She wouldn't be here long, the place was a temporary stopover, but he'd done the same for every window in the apartment, and bought and installed a security bar on the front door, too. Not that he expected her to have trouble, but Jock was a big fan of planning ahead. "Bar food, but I heard at the hardware store they've got the best burger in town."

"High praise from this stranger I've never met." Her voice was a teasing lilt, and he rolled his eyes and kept moving through the apartment into the kitchen.

Silly stood unwrapping the final box of dishes, stacking them in the dishwasher. Which he didn't understand. She'd washed them after taking them from her old cabinets but before packing them up, and now was washing them before putting them in her new cabinets.

"Bob's a good guy. You'd like him. I'll introduce you. He's full of local stories and lore." Jock slipped in behind her and bent to press his lips to her shoulder, dragging the kiss up her neck to the edge of her jaw. She angled her head to flash him a smile, then arched her neck in invitation. "Wanna go have a beer with your man and then come home and get lucky?"

"I could be convinced." He waited until she'd finished with the last dish, then lifted the dishwasher door with one toe as he wrapped his arms around her middle, hoisting her at the same time he closed the door. "*Jock.*"

"I know you're hungry." He adjusted his grip, turning and bringing her higher against his chest so she could give him her mouth. He worked for a whimper, and when he got one, smiled against her lips. "I wanna feed my woman." She scoffed and he chuckled. "And I wanna do that, then come home with my woman, and get laid."

"In that case." She gave a wiggle, and he stooped and set her feet on the floor. "Lemme wash my face." He watched her walk away as he dug out his phone. After the last phone call with Gunny, he'd shifted his questions to Mason. Not only was the man intelligent and sympathetic, but he'd founded the Rebels, and Jock knew out of pride for the organization, Mason would not steer him wrong. He also didn't want to have that same conversation, so he led with a text.

Protocol question: I'm here in IMC territory. Wear my colors to a bar, not theirs but biker friendly, or not?

The response was immediate and to the point.

You do that check-in I told you to do?

He had not. Jock sighed and started typing, paused and backspaced, started typing again. His phone dinged, and he saw Mason had added to their conversation.

You didn't do it. Do it now. Like I told you before, we're friendly, not allies but close to. You show respect and check in, then wear your patch, and all's good.

Jock didn't hesitate this time, just responded with a simple: **Got it**

He scrolled up the thread, found the phone number Mason had texted him three days ago, tapped it, and put the phone to his ear.

"Ayeap?" Like all the voices down here, even that simple drawn-out word was musical.

"Pony?" He received an affirmative grunt in response. Pony was the Sargent at Arms for the Incoherent MC and the approach from any outside club. In person or via any other method, if you didn't know another member personally, and sometimes even if you did, an officer was who you reached out to. Protocol. Just like his next statement. Instead of leading with a name-dropping rendition of who he knew, he told him who he was, leading with the most important information. "I'm a member of the Rebel Wayfarers Fort Wayne chapter. Jock. I'm in town and wanted to pay my respects to the IMC."

Proving he knew exactly the club Jock was part of, Pony didn't waste any time getting to business. "RWMC got official business down here on IMC's patch of dirt?"

"Nope. My girl's moving to Hammond. I brought her down. Wanted to take her out tonight, but wanted to pay respect first."

"RWMC got an ole lady movin' to town, sounds to me like that's business. You want to revise your original ask?"

"Not official business. My business. Me and her are going to work things out, but how that works out is yet to be determined."

Pony scoffed. "Man, you put a PO in my territory, that makes it official business even if you don't think it does. Mason shoulda taught you that."

He knew the tension and pain bled through his voice now, but he couldn't stop it. Leaving Silly, even if he'd determined to make it temporary, was still tearing at him. "Mason's the one who gave me your number. My girl doesn't have a vest. I was going to petition for one—why am I going into this for you? Jesus, all I want to do is take my girl out for burgers at Trudette's." Jock sighed. "I'd be obliged if you'd pass on my respects. I don't have but a couple more days here with her before I gotta roll back north. Deke's bought a bike from one of your brothers, and I'm ridin' it home."

"Take your girl to Trudette's. Get her a burger. Tell 'em Pony sent you." Jock breathed easier at that, because it meant he'd been heard. That was good, and now he could report back to Mason that he'd checked in and everything was fine. "See you in thirty. Save a couple of seats."

Jock froze, heard nothing more, and pulled the phone away to see the call had disconnected. Tension bunched the muscles in his shoulders and back.

Shit.

***

He'd selected a corner booth in the back, one with a direct line of sight to the door—and, through the windows, to the main parking lot. There were a few bikes outside now, but when he'd stood at the doorway under the premise of waiting for a nonexistent hostess, he'd verified none of the patches at the tables were IMC.

Incoherent MC was the dominant in the region. Their mother chapter was here in Hammond, and he should have known that, according to Mason's curt follow-up texts. IMC had many close allies, including another dom club just to the east, the Caddo Hobos MC, better known as the CoBos. IMC as a club was strong, with more than a dozen chapters, and vigorously defended its territory against all comers. Mason had repeated that last bit.

He'd also included that the club had his respect, which said a fuck of a lot. That didn't stop Jock from sweating whatever meeting this was that Pony had demanded. Twisted was IMC national president, but he was also based here in Hammond, so he could conceivably be here tonight, too. That would be fucked, because as a member, he really shouldn't talk to officers of another club. But the IMC's SAA had ordered Jock to hold a couple of seats, and as a guest in their territory, he was. The booth was big, and he'd crowded Silly into the same side as him, backs to the wall, leaving the other bench empty.

She'd listened carefully as he filled her in on the ten-minute drive. Around clubs more than half her life, she understood everything he said and all the things he didn't. That meant she hadn't demanded his arm around her, wasn't clinging to his hand. She had her hand on his thigh and was pressed close, but not so close he couldn't get at his pistol if needed. He just hoped like fuck it wouldn't come to that.

The waitress had just walked away from the table with their order when he heard it. Heard them coming. It was a rolling wall of sound, so many bike exhausts in a group that the tones overlapped and merged into a single rumble. It died down in fits and starts, small at first, then big chunks of the noise cut out at a time as men backed their bikes into parking spaces and killed the engines. Through the window, he watched a wave of black surge towards the diner, slowly separating into individuals, the black interspersed with color he recognized as women. Some wearing a vest, no doubt POs, but a lot of tank tops and tees, just like Silly.

Jock blew out a deep breath, then pulled in another, relaxing the smallest amount.

They'd brought their women. That didn't say meet; that said night out at a local bar.

He heard them before the door opened, loud shouts of laughter, rumbling conversations. Then they swept inside and the first eight or so arrowed straight towards his booth, the rest spreading out through the room. Jock patted Silly's leg in a directive to stay planted, and he shoved out of the booth and unfolded, waiting at the end of the table.

Nameplates declared Twisted—which was his worst nightmare made flesh, having to deal one-on-one with a national president. He'd read Pony, Busk, and Po'Boy, where a difference in colored nameplates caught his eye, then came to Wrench—heart racing, he racked his memory because that name stood out. As did Ace, standing next to the man. Two women, one definitely pregnant, stood directly behind two of the men, Twisted and Wrench.

As he'd been instructed, Jock kept his lips sealed, waiting for IMC to break the silence.

Twisted nodded, flicked the briefest glance behind him at Silly, and did a double take. Gaze back to Jock, he made a show of looking up, exaggerating the angle of his neck, so it wasn't a surprise that he led with "Jesus, fuck me twice, you are one *big* dude." Teeth flashed in the man's beard, and Jock let his lips twitch in response. There'd been no introduction, so he kept his silence. "Like the addition, man. Old school is appreciated here." Twisted pointed a finger at the large safety pin fastened just above Jock's nameplate. As Mason had told it, this was a symbol that a biker wearing colors was just moving through territory. Not a surety to keep confrontations at bay, but a help he'd sworn by. Seemed Mason was right.

Twisted shoved his hand out and Jock reciprocated, surprised when the man went for his thumb instead of a shake, but he allowed himself to be drawn forwards and took the pounding against his outer shoulder, also reciprocating, careful to not touch the leather of the man's vest. "Twisted, man. Well met."

"Jock. Back atcha." He tried not to let his relief show and knew he'd failed when Po'Boy flashed him an insolent grin. "Alla y'all."

"I'm IMC." Twisted said this just like Mason had often said the same, claiming the club in a way any man paying attention could not mistake. "That reprobate there is my ride-or-die, Po'Boy, no matter he's done patched out of IMC." The statement was puzzling, but Jock watched as, thumb over his shoulder, Twisted didn't have to turn and look to see where the man was, trusting he'd be at his back. "You talked to Pony, and we nabbed a couple others to sit with us. Busk here sold your boy Deke his latest build, and the man wanted to see who'd be babyin' that beast to the cold, cold north." He faked a shiver that made everyone laugh. "But," he worked to drag this word out long, and Jock braced even as Twisted gave his hand a reassuring squeeze, "we had visitors and couldn't rightly run out on them. So we let the CoBos tag along with. Wrench is their nat prez, and Ace is the past." He leaned close and, in a stage-whisper, asked, "You intimidated yet, man?"

"Not yet. I'm a Rebel." That came out far cockier than he felt, but it was the right move because Twisted stared up at him, that split in his beard wider, more white showing through. Then the man threw back his head and laughed.

"Fucking spades, man. I'm gonna like you." Twisted gave his hand another tug and a squeeze, and yanked him in for a one-armed clinch just like Gunny or Mason would. Jock allowed it, and followed the man's lead to pound his back twice, on the leather but still well away from the patch. Friendly, not far from being allies, but not brothers. He stepped back and Jock released his hold. "Now shove the fuck over, and we'll take a load off. I'm hungry, and I've recognized your girl there. I got some questions for her."

Glancing back at Silly, she gave him a tiny nod as she scooted to the far end of the bench. *Fuck.* This was going to jack with him. On the inside like that, men he didn't know pinning him in? He swallowed hard and held her gaze. It didn't take long, a flash of a second, and she realized what was happening, reversing her course until she shimmied out of the booth and stood beside him. She offered the women a wave first, then lifted her eyes to Twisted before returning her gaze to Jock. "I'll be back in a minute. I need to visit the facilities. Save me a spot?" That gave him a reason to let the other men slide in first, so he stepped back, taking her with him. He bent deep, touched his mouth to hers and nodded.

By the time he'd turned back to the table, both benches were full and Twisted had pulled two chairs up at the end. He was sprawled on one, the petite redhead who'd been behind him perched on his thigh. Jock accepted the other chair and sat, only then realizing Twisted had given him the one that allowed him a wall nearly at his back. Just like Gunny had done the first time they'd met, Twisted had somehow read his reluctance, understood it wasn't disrespect driving it, and given him enough room to be comfortable.

Po'Boy was to his right, and Jock gave him a nod. Next to him was a blonde, and then Wrench. That seemed backwards, because the national president of the CoBos wouldn't normally be pinned in like that. Busk, Pony, and Ace sat in the opposite seat, backs to the room.

Twisted made a noise and Jock swung to look at him. "Your girl." Twisted paused a beat. "She's the tattoo chick." Jock nodded. "She's good." He smiled that time as he nodded. "You got any examples to show?"

"Yeap, she's working on a big back piece for me." He smiled, knowing the expression was filled with pride. "Her original, start to finish. We've worked in the outline, now gotta pin her down to do the rest for me." He gestured towards the scars on his throat. "It took some contemplation, but now we've started, I find I'm anxious to get it done. Have her on me like she wants."

Twisted sighed and gave him a slow nod, head tipping towards Jock. "You served."

It wasn't a question, but he answered anyway. "I did."

"Gratitude for your service, brother." Jock jerked his gaze to Ace, who'd spoken from his seat farthest away. "What branch?"

"Oorah." Jock grinned when the man echoed the sound. "Marines. You?"

"Hooah. Army." Ace grinned back. "My tours were in a different country, but damn I respect you boys for taking on that sandbox."

Jock felt his smile fade. "Thank you for your service," and then he gave the man back the word that meant the world, "brother." Silly's warm hand slipped up his shoulder to the back of his neck, and he wrapped her up, bringing her in to sit crossways in his lap. "Gonna have to eat like this, baby."

"I'll manage." She pushed up and pressed her lips to the hinge of his jaw. "You good?" she whispered, and he nodded. "Good." Turning in his arms, she looked between the two women, gauging their standing in the club, and shook her head. "I'm stuck here, ladies. You're equals. So I'll go first. I'm Silly." She paused, and Jock chuckled at the expressions on their faces, clearly waiting for her to continue.

"That's her name. She does that shit to everyone."

Grinning, the redhead giggled. "I'm Penny." She pointed to the blonde. "That's Crissy. I'm Twisted's, as you can see." The man in question smacked his hand hard on her ass, and she grinned wider. Then he curled his arm around to cradle her stomach, and her expression gentled. "Crissy belongs to Po'Boy and Wrench."

From the intense stare Twisted turned his direction, Jock knew this was a test, just as sure as the heavy firepower of so many officers showing for a meal with him was. He nodded, tipped his head down to catch Silly's gaze and said loud enough for all to hear, "Sounds like those boys got it goin' on, baby."

"No, Jock. My man's got it goin' on." She thrust her hand between her legs and cupped his crotch, his dick twitching when she gave him a squeeze before turning back to Penny. "Pleased to finally meet you. You're quite the legend." She angled her head to look at Crissy, and he heard the grin in her voice as she said, "And sister, you are someone I'd like to have a chat with sometime. I bet you're a hoot to party with."

"To be clear." Po'Boy's voice was low and rough, riding the edge of mean even in this setting. "We're all three together. Him," he tipped his head towards Wrench, who Jock saw was rolling his eyes, "me," Po'Boy jerked a thumb towards his own chest, "and her." Tipping his body sideways, he crowded against Crissy. "Together."

"Pleased you got that, man." Jock nodded, holding his gaze, not giving an inch. "Takes a solid pairing to withstand the pressure in any conditions, but to hold fast to what you've got? Rock. You'll get nothing but respect from me."

"I like him." Wrench flashed him a lazy grin, then captured one of Po'Boy's hands and confidently threaded his fingers through. "Not as much as I like you, babe."

"You better fuckin' not," Po'Boy shot back, then turned to face Jock. "And you better not get any fuckin' ideas. Don't matter how much you," his voice lifted, turning falsetto as he mimicked Silly's words, "got it goin' on."

"My woman's all I want or need." He didn't miss how Silly melted into him more. "But thanks for the vote of confidence."

"Oh, I like him, too." Twisted was laughing as he banged a fist on the table. "Beer, burgers, and brothers. Ain't no shit better'n that shit."

"Can we talk about pussy for a change? Or bikes? Or fuck, I don't know. Golf?" Pony tipped his head backwards and spoke to the ceiling. "I'm done talkin' about cock. And not all of us have an ole lady to go home to."

"And whose fault is that?" Po'Boy jumped on the new topic with both feet. "Yours, motherfucker. I set you up with that chick last week."

"Fuckin' RC mama? Were you serious? She's been passed around half a dozen weekend warrior groups, man. You're an asshole of a friend."

"But we're friends." Po'Boy leaned forwards and tapped the table with one finger. "We *are* friends. Is that confirmation? Because since I patched into the CoBos, you ain't been actin' friendly."

"Fuck you, we're friends." Pony leaned in, too, and tapped the tabletop with two fingers. "Always been friends, always gonna be friends. That shit was settled solid, right fucking here, brother. It don't matter what patch you wear, I'm with Twisted on that. You're more than my friend, man. You're my *brother*."

Silence settled around the table, heavy and dark, and Jock glanced from face to face, reading sorrow and grief there. The waitress chose that moment to step in, and she must have known these men's preferences, because without them having ordered, she settled mugs and cans of beer all around. Then, understanding the mood of the table, she beat a fast retreat.

Twisted moved first, leaning forwards to grip a can of pop, which he passed to Penny, then a can of beer, which shocked Jock when he passed it to Silly. Po'Boy held a mug out to Jock, and he accepted it wordlessly. When all the drinks had been claimed, Twisted lifted his high and, without turning around, shouted, "A toast." The sound level in the room dropped immediately, and he filled it with another shout. "To Jimbo, Scot, Doobie, Astro, Hopper, Cajun, Chevy, and Wheels. Ride in paradise." His words were followed by a rumbling echo of "ride in paradise" from every corner of the room.

Jock and Silly lifted their beers and, taking their cues from the people surrounding them, drank deeply.

"Had a war start here." Twisted nodded towards the booth. "We lost eight men that day. Seven died right fuckin' here, at this table, including my papaw, Jimbo."

"Jesus, Twisted. I didn't know."

"Nor should you. This is IMC lore, not RWMC. Pony was here, saw it go down, assisted. He was Vicar's Wrath at the time, SAA of their 9th Ward chapter. We fuckin' gutted that club and took it down. Now the only VWMC patches you see are a poor replica, and the men worth knowin' and having at a body's back wear my patch or Wrench's." He lifted his beer again, and every man at the table matched the gesture, echoing his "To Papaw."

"Jimbo was IMC president and founder. Him, Ace over there, who founded the CoBos, and two others who ain't suckin' air no more served overseas. They came back, started their clubs, and here we are." Twisted gestured towards the table, then tipped his head backwards, indicating the rest of the men and women who'd come with him. "We represent those four clubs, and four more. Eight clubs, now consolidated into two cooperative and allied dominants. Shit happens, it gets real, and we fuckin' deal."

"RWMC lore is much the same." Jock stuck to the facts anyone could know if they researched it. "Officers could give you deeper information, but we started in Chicago under an asshole as the Rebel Fiends. Mason took the gavel and birthed the club anew as the RWMC. Along the way, as I've heard it, since I've only been in the club a couple of years, he pulled in about a dozen clubs. The members who were worth a shit wear the skull and key. The ones who weren't?" He shrugged. "Nobody fuckin' cares."

Silence, broken only by the laughter and clinking of tableware from other tables, then Twisted sighed. "We done got deep and dark." Head bent to Penny, Twisted cut his eyes towards Jock. "Was not my intention, man."

"Shit happens." He made a so-what gesture.

"Still, not my intent. I wanted to meet the man Mason felt comfortable sending on my patch without a brother at his back. Then—" He flashed a smile at Silly. "I recognized you, pretty lady. You're my new shop manager."

She stilled on Jock's lap but didn't respond. He studied Twisted's face and saw a flash of humor there, so Jock held his peace, waiting.

"Not *my* manager, per se." Twisted stroked his beard. "But that shop's been IMC's since the day the door opened. Jasper, the old owner? He was the shit, man. We kept it safe and clean, because everyone knew if you fucked with Jasper, you fucked with us. Got my first tat in Jasper's chair." He shoved back in his chair, going from sprawling to leaning forwards in a second, Penny cradled to his chest. "I'd be honored to sit in your chair, Sylvia Perez."

What the actual fuck?

***

Silly

Head tipped to rest on Jock's shoulder, she felt his hand at her hip tighten, fingers digging in. This wasn't a threat, wasn't even the precursor to one, not as out in the open as this was, and while she'd be pissed at Ernie not sharing history, she also wasn't surprised. He'd been existing on the fringes of a dominant club for so long, he'd probably forgotten how it was when territories rubbed up against each other. Or in this case, when people moved into a territory that could be construed as an initial foray. She let her lips curl slightly, watching as Twisted noted even that.

"You know who I am." He nodded, lifted his beer to his mouth and took a long drink. "All my history?"

His gaze sharpened, and he rested the mug on Penny's thigh, where she automatically wrapped her fingers around it, as if this was something they did all the time. "You got more history than the show and working for Ernesto?"

Jock choked and coughed, trying to cover his snort of laughter, but she knew he hadn't done a good job when Twisted's sharp gaze grew even sharper, more intense. There was an intelligence behind those eyes she could appreciate, and it spoke to his being here right now as more of a big move than she'd initially thought.

"You seem to know my name." Not a question, but Twisted nodded anyway. "My *full* name?" She emphasized the second word, and let her tone climb on the last, then waited a beat while he stared at her before shaking his head. With a smile, she gave it to him, wondering if he'd catch the important part that would tell him it was more than the RWMC sitting in his backyard. "Sylvia Rene Anna Estavez Perez."

Backing up that intelligence she'd recognized, he didn't take even a second to bark out "What the fuck?"

Silly patted the air in a calming gesture she knew would have enraged Mason, so she wasn't shocked when it bore the same fruit here. *Better to keep him off balance for a moment longer.* "Yes, yes. That branch of the family is unfortunately well known." She shrugged, giving him a "what can you do" gesture.

"Estavez." He scraped his top teeth against his tongue, as if he'd tasted something foul. "Which brother do you claim?"

"Raul has always been my favorite cousin." The furrow between his brows didn't lessen, so she gave him a little more. "Family is complicated, and you probably already know the deep history between Carlos and the Rebels, with Slate and Watcher first, then with Chicago entire?" He lifted his chin in acknowledgment. "His wife was sent to kill me. So tell me, friend, how do you think my relations with that side of the family went? She was my blood cousin, Raul is my near."

"He keep tabs on you?" She shook her head and Twisted scoffed. "Bullshit. Man keeps his finger in everything he can."

"He does not." She paused, then smiled because he would also understand this. "Carmela, however, does."

"Fucking hell." That came from Po'Boy, seated to the side, and she turned to look at him. "You mean we're liable to have her here to visit you, and you know that'll bring her daddy's soldiers with it."

"Unlikely," Jock interjected. "Public knowledge, so I'm not speakin' out of school, but she's spending time with her old man these days out in Cali. Not her daddy, but—"

"Hurley," Twisted interrupted. "Yeah, we got the fuckin' brief on that shit. Jesus, man, you claim you aren't bringing heat to my patch, but from where I sit, it looks like the kitchen's about to get fucking enflamed. You are fuckin' in the wrong patch, man."

Silly rested her hand on Jock's arm, feeling the tension in his muscles everywhere they touched. "We aren't fucking with you. And the interest you're worried about that might turn this way, shouldn't. And if it does, it isn't intentional. I don't expect *anything* to come this way. It's been a while since I even saw Mela, she's so busy building a life."

There was a weighty silence for a moment, then Twisted tipped his head back and sighed heavily. Chin down, he focused on them, then drawled, "Jock, my man." Twisted took his beer back from Penny and lifted it towards where Silly sat in Jock's lap. "You're gonna make things interestin', that's a for sure truth."

"Told you my man had it goin' on." She pushed to get just enough sassy into her words, and as the table erupted in laughter, she smiled brightly at them.

I'll take it.

Have It All

Jock

"He was IMC until recently, right?" Jock's question was directed to Busk. By invitation from Twisted, which Jock knew was more of a command they present themselves, he and Silly had shown at the IMC clubhouse, following the mass of bikes from Trudette's. They were in the big backyard, and he was standing around one of several barrels filled with ice and beer. It was too hot to have fires going, but there were flickering tiki torches staked in the ground all around the outer boundaries of the space, the pungent scent of citronella thick in the air. He and

Busk had been talking bikes and builds, something Jock could spend all day doing. Po'Boy had just walked by with a nod for them, and Jock had watched him go directly to where Wrench was standing next to Twisted. "That's gotta be a tough path to walk. Old loyalties at war with new."

"Couple of months now. Still new, but he's makin' it work." Busk chuckled. "Probably easier than you'd think, because CoBos do not expect him to take sides. They made him non-voting for a year, which means he's got no sway."

"He's sharing the bed of the nat prez." Jock shrugged. "That's sway."

"Nah, Wrench was born and bred for this, man. He's got his own way and is true to it. Good man." Busk nodded. "Good brother, no matter the patch he wears."

"I keep hearing that phrase and it boggles the mind."

"Why? Brotherhood is why we seek a club. Shouldn't be too much to expect that a change in circumstances would not change that need. We surround ourselves with brothers who love the wind, and draw family lines around that with our patch brothers. Would you sentence a man to do without family?" With a slow head shake, Busk asked him, "What is it you think gets in the way?"

"Fuck, man. Loyalty?" Even being here felt odd, as if he were walking on eggshells. Just knowing he represented the RWMC had him sweating every word that came out of his mouth. The idea of bestowing that loyalty on a different club didn't make sense. Like changing teams in the middle of a game. "I don't know. Every club's different, from what I see. How can a body fit into one and then turn and fit into another? They're gonna have different vibes, or...fuck, I don't know. Styles. They're distinct, so how does it work?"

"You think because she's brown that's gonna be a problem?" Jock's head jerked back, because Silly's race hadn't crossed his mind. It wasn't even on his radar around the Rebels, no matter the chapter. "Don't. Because we got brothers of color, and we got brothers with ole ladies of color. And if that ain't it, then is it you? You got a problem with a club that accepted a gay officer?"

Jock chuckled at that, a picture of Myron and Mouse slow dancing at the Fort Wayne chapter's holiday party flashing in his head. "Pretty sure your man's bi, and no, I don't have a problem with that."

"Gay, bi, whatever it is, you think the club should've had a problem with it?" Even if it was in a friendly way, it seemed Busk was baiting him. Jock relaxed because the man wouldn't get far that way.

He let his lip wrinkle in annoyance. "Gay and bi are different." No sense withholding what was common knowledge. "I know. We got a gay national treasurer, and I'm pretty sure he has never looked at pussy. Your man over there, Po'Boy, he's all about Crissy just as much as he is Wrench." Jock stifled a snort. "I'd think badly of a club that kicked a good brother to the curb over something like that. Good for you, IMC seems smart."

Busk seemed to stifle a noise far back in his throat and then laughed loudly. When he sobered, he clapped Jock on the shoulder and muttered, "Well said, brother. Well said." After a moment Busk nodded and tipped his chin to point across the lot. "Your woman's makin' friends."

Jock looked the direction he indicated, seeing the man was right. Silly was occupying one half of an old-style metal glider, turned sideways to face Penny, who, he'd learned, regardless of the fact that she was only weeks away from giving birth, had nearly as wild a streak as Silly did. They were gabbing like hens, leaned in close. Penny's bootheel dug deep in the dirt, keeping the glider moving back and forth, slow and steady. Silly threw back her head and laughed, much as he'd seen her do with Sharon, or Willa, two of the Rebel women with whom she was tight.

"That's good." Jock felt another band of tension unknot in his muscles. She needed friends, needed people to bond with, and it would make him feel a thousand times better knowing there'd be someone she could call while he was gone. "This whole day's been good. I love her so fuckin' much." He gestured to the yard filled with pockets of men and women, children dashing around. "I didn't realize how much I'd been missing this."

"Company of good brothers, good liquor, and a good woman." Twisted's voice came from beside him, and Jock instinctively stuck out his hand as he turned, greeting the man the same way he would any of the Rebels. Twisted clasped Jock's wrist and pulled him in, fist thudding his back. "The secret to a good life."

"You know it." Jock stepped back, making room for Twisted and another IMC member he'd met earlier, Wildman. The name was familiar, but he wasn't sure why.

"I'm gonna be plain as I know how to be." Twisted's gaze pinned him to the spot, and Jock startled, the ferocity of the expression on the man's face unexpected after the warm welcome he and Silly had enjoyed. "RWMC patch cannot move to my piece of ground. That will not stand." Jock nodded and opened his mouth, but Twisted cut him off with a gesture. "That's gonna leave you three options, as I see it. You wanna hear what I see?"

Staring down at the man, Twisted's clear, intelligent eyes holding Jock's gaze, he felt an unexpected anger building inside him. He knew this was just one way of how clubs worked, but the idea that this man thought he could keep him and Silly apart was ludicrous. He was a guest on their property, in their territory, and they'd been respectful, not asking him to pack his colors and not asking him if he was carrying, making it clear he was being given the same consideration they did allies and friends. He took a deep, deep breath, straightened his spine, and nodded, bracing for whatever would come.

Twisted didn't waste any time. "First, you can go splitsville with that pretty lady, and be the loser for not having her in your life."

"Not gonna happen." Jock kept it from a shout, but only barely, his words coming out firm and strong.

"Figured as much." Twisted glanced towards where his Penny and Jock's Silly sat. "Next option is you can take her and go back home."

Another response that took zero thought, because he'd already agonized over the decision for too long. "Also not happening. This is huge for her, and I'd be no partner if I didn't back her in this."

"Good answer," Wildman put in. "If there's a choice to be made, always, but always play to pussy."

"Shut the fuck up, man." Twisted turned and shot a glare at Wildman. "I'm workin' here."

From his grin, Jock knew Wildman's words were a lie. "Sorry, boss. My bad. Won't happen again."

Twisted opened his mouth, but Wildman beat him to it. "Promise, boss. Won't happen."

"Three, and if my brother will shut the fuck up and let me get to the meat of it." Another glare for Wildman was met with a wider grin. "You patch over."

Heart pounding in his chest, Jock found his voice failed him.

I'm a Rebel.

Over the heads of the other men, he saw Silly looking in their direction. She captured his gaze, wrinkled her nose, and pursed her lips in a kiss blown over the flattened palm of one hand.

He'd started his life over when he'd chosen to stay in Fort Wayne. Separated from the military, divorced, and homeless, he'd been rootless until he found Tank, and with his recovered dog came Gunny and his family, and with Gunny came his brothers. Jock remembered the days and nights of getting to know the men, and it had gone just about like today and tonight had. Different personalities and different faces, but the same sense of exploring the possibility of a brotherhood.

Eyes still fixed on him, Silly tipped her head, wild hair flowing over one shoulder, and she screwed up her face in a frown. He gave her a chin lift, and the concern eased from her expression. She wanted something good for him, just as much as he wanted the shop to be a blowout success.

I can have it all.

Choosing his words with care, he slowly voiced something that would tell Twisted where his head was, without overstepping his role here or as a member of the Rebel Wayfarers MC. "I'm thinkin' the next questions I have, I should direct them to my president." Jock tore his gaze from Silly and cut a glance at Twisted, taking in the serious look on the man's face. One final burning question burst from him, his desire for brotherhood making his mouth rash. "But what you're sayin' is you'd have me?"

"Would take a vote." Twisted shrugged as if he'd expected the question all along. Which he may have. "But if I'm backin' you?" He angled a finger towards Jock on the "you" and back to himself for the next statement. "If I'm the one making the goddamned approach like I am right the fuck now? I heard you were smart, Jock. What the fuck do you think?"

"I'd sponsor." Busk spoke from beside him, overlapping Pony's growled, "He could be my recruit."

"Man, we wouldn't make him prospect." Wildman drew in a snorting laugh. "Limited member, six months. And I think, given his history, and what I got goin' on with all my shit? Oh yeah. He'd need to be mine." He threw back his head and crowed, then bizarrely shouted, "Quack, quack."

"Quack fuckin' quack. Motherfucking asshole." Jock saw Po'Boy coming their way, Wrench at his shoulder. "Fucking IMC always getting in the way of what I wanna do. Dammit, Twisted, did you already make a spiel? Did you make your pitch while my back was fuckin' turned? Goddamn motherfucker. You did, didn't you?"

Twisted's beard split and white shone through. "Ayeap."

"Goddammit to fucking hell. I wanted him for CoBos." Po'Boy's scowl was fierce. "Why the fuck would you do that?"

"Uh, mebbe because I'm standing on Incoherent right fuckin' now. Why wouldn't I do that? You ever know me to go easy?" Twisted's returning scowl was made a lie by the genuine amusement in his tone. "I ain't one who reckons things like that. My patch, my ground, my pitch."

The quick back-and-forth soothed Jock as the easy comfort between these men rose. This was a brotherhood, like what the Rebels had.

No maybes about it. If I want it, I can have this.

He knew Mason wouldn't naysay him. Not over this.

Jock could have it all.

***

Silly

She'd been watching him closely, a churn in her gut that said IMC inviting them here, nearly strong-arming Jock to drive her car to the clubhouse after leaving Trudette's, they'd have an ulterior motive. Penny had eased her mind slightly with just how open and welcoming she'd been, free with hilarious stories about her "boys" as she called them, a term that seemed to encompass the entirety of the IMC and CoBos memberships.

With her uncle being one of the CoBos founders and an officer back under Ace's rule, both men she'd spoken of with great affection, Penny straddled two clubs in a more direct way than Silly did. Somehow Penny'd managed to hook her wagon to Twisted, the powerhouse of a club president that not whispers but shouts had reached Chicago about. He'd taken on not one but two clubs at the same time, gone to war and come out the other side a legend.

With an eye roll, Penny had verified some of the more fantastic stories that Silly had discounted, and even now, looking at Twisted standing there talking to Jock, she could not process how the man and woman had lived through what happened and made their way together to this.

The stress and strain she'd watched build on Jock's face were slowly bleeding away, comfort and ease taking their place. Whatever was going to happen had happened, and he wasn't walking away. He gave her his eyes again, and his face softened, his expression going sweet when she blew him another kiss.

"It's going to be okay." Penny's soft words struck Silly hard, and she turned to stare at the woman. Hair as wild as Silly's was on any given day, Penny's was a brilliant, strong auburn that said she'd earned her given name early. "On the way to Trudette's, Twisted was shouting back and forth with Po'Boy, arguing who'd get to have him. Po'Boy got distracted and Twisted got in there first. I'm going to say that with this happening, you should prepare to have your man movin' here sooner rather than later."

"I just want him to be good. He's steady with his brothers, loves the work at the garage, and if I'm in his bed, we'll beat back his dreams." She saw two more men make their way to where he stood, hands outstretched for a shake and introduction, and a moment later, she heard the gruff tones of the three men in a shared "Oorah."

"It'll be good, Silly. Swear. If IMC isn't a fit, CoBos aren't far, and Ace is already pissed he didn't get a clear shot at talking him over. Ace's strong and steady, and I love him like he's my uncle, but when he shines brightest is while working with the men coming back from overseas." Penny reached out and wrapped her fingers around Silly's forearm. "If you're good, your man'll be good."

Silly took a deep breath, did a little shimmy to shrug off the tension that had built in her limbs, and shared, "The shop is beyond expectation, and if Jock's happy, then I'm happy."

Penny smiled at her, her expression brilliant and pleased. "He'll be happy because you will be."

"I'll work my ass off to make it so." Silly felt her chin lift as she made this promise.

"And that's why it'll be just like I laid it out." Penny's grin didn't lessen, didn't falter, and Silly found herself returning it.

"You're a hoot, woman."

***

Jock

"Jock." Silly's cry was soft, rising to a keen on his next thrust. The quaver rolling through her tone made his cock jerk in response. "Baby."

Jock wrapped his fingers around her waist, her silken, inked skin hot under his touch. She sagged towards his chest, head hanging as she clenched hard around him, lost in the bliss he was giving her. The sleek glide of her pussy was glorious torture as her pace remained steady at a slow and maddening rate. "Silly, I need to move, baby. Want to watch you take me."

"Just a few more…" She trailed off as she rose and fell over him again, panting out his name when he tipped his hips, working a different angle. "Jock, my God." She tightened around him in waves, her pussy rippling as it milked his cock.

Done with waiting, he didn't give her any warning, taking the necessary steps to rev things to a higher level. Heels to the mattress, he spread his knees and powered up into her, lifting and dropping her onto his shaft while the orgasm continued rolling through her. He watched her nipples tighten, pebbling into rosy peaks, and felt his balls draw up when she offered a soft moan. Her fingers were spread across his chest, holding herself in place, as he fucked her from underneath. Three or four minutes passed, his breath coming ragged and fast, and her head lifted. Eyes bright, she dug her nails into his skin and tensed her legs, taking over the act of rising and falling, taking his cock.

"There, baby," he grunted, gaze fixed on her face, watching as the daze washed away slowly. She caught her bottom lip in her teeth, rolled it out slowly, and nodded, kicking up the pace. "I'm right fuckin' there."

She nodded and took it when he thrust up and held himself rooted inside her as far as he could get, grinding their hips together, the walls of her pussy fluttering as he pulled another pulse of pleasure from her. Knifing up, he sat and wrapped an arm around her back, pulling her close and dipping his mouth to her tit before he sucked hard, drawing her deep.

"Jock." Her lips grazed his temple.

"Love you, baby." He released his hold on her to give her those words, smiling against her skin when she tightened around him. "You like hearing it."

"I love knowing it," she returned, and he tipped his head up and captured her lips, kissing her like she was the sweetest taste he'd ever had in his mouth, because she was.

Only The Best

Jock

"Did you see my sister?" That was Mason's first question when Jock video-called the next morning.

Jock paused, wondering at the brusque tone. "No, should I have?"

"You remember Justine went missing and was rescued?" Jock flinched at the memory of the tense faces around the clubhouse, half a dozen men riding out like the devil was chasing them. Mason nodded at his reaction and gave Jock another piece of a puzzle he didn't know he needed. "Wildman was that rescue."

"No shit?" Mason shook his head, face solemn. *Jesus.* That tie spoke volumes and underscored the tense desire the IMC had in pulling Jock into the fold. "I knew it was IMC but didn't hear the particulars. The man's name was familiar, but I didn't put it together. There a reason they're keeping a low profile?"

"She's keeping it quiet until she can bow out from her job. But then, she's assured me she's gonna be in Hammond for good." Mason smiled, and the fondness on his face tugged at Jock's heartstrings. "Be good for her. She had a man who wasn't afraid to take her in hand and keep her from doin' stupid-ass shit like get kidnapped." His gaze sharpened. "I hear Wildman's that man. What's your take on him?"

"Solid. Man is solid and respected by both IMC and CoBos." He grinned as he remembered the rising calls of "Quack, quack," finally explained by Busk. "Justine could do worse." A thought struck him, and he hummed for a moment then observed, "That'll be all the women in your life hooked up with bikers, though. How you feel about that?"

"Man, Dolly is not old enough to hook up, and thank God for that shit. But when she is, if she does?" Mason smiled that soft smile again. *Good to see him so happy.* "Long as he's good to her, you think I'll give a shit?"

Oh, that was a fuckin' lie. Jock couldn't let it pass, needing to get at least one harmless dig in. "I dunno, boss. I heard hella stories about your fight to keep Bethy and Fury apart."

"Different days, brother. Different days." Mason lifted his chin. "Now, to the matter you called about. How long do I get to keep you?"

"What?" *How the hell would he know what I'm thinking?* Jock shook his head. "What do you mean?"

"How long, Jock? You got three builds goin', and Red's already pissed that he's had to put off that shit. You want Bear to pick 'em up and finish, or you comin' back to tidy your shit?" Mason gestured off camera, and Gunny stalked into frame, already glowering at Jock. "Gunny's offered to be your beatout."

Jock remembered the look on Silly's face when she blew him that kiss. Remembered her riding his dick last night after they got home, and that was before he told her about the offer he'd gotten. And he also remembered the hope and cautious excitement in her eyes when he did recount his conversations. *Be worth it,* he thought. *Be worth anything.*

Squaring his shoulders, he stared at the two men for a moment, then took a hard breath. "If it's gotta go that way, I'll come back just for the beatout." He swallowed and nodded, throat tight. "I'll finish my builds, too, if you'll let me."

"Jesus, brother." Gunny's guttural words tore a hole through him. "Fuck, man, you know I'm from there, right?"

"Hammond?" Gunny dipped his chin to his throat, and Jock let his head swing slowly back and forth, never losing sight of Gunny's pained expression. "No, I didn't."

"Near enough. My granny's buried in Acadia Parish." Gunny's scowl deepened, brows drawing together. "We're really going to lose you?"

"It's the only way I can see keepin' Silly how I want to keep her." Jock pressed his face closer to the phone, needing Gunny of all people to understand. "I love her, Lane. Moon and back, she's it for me."

"I know, Jake. See it on your face every time you look at her. I get it, man. I totally get it." Gunny blew out a harsh breath. "Don't mean it doesn't suck ass like a motherfucker, but I get it."

"Twisted called me." Mason had stepped back while Gunny and Jock talked, but he took his place beside Gunny again now. "Before he went to Trudette's, he called me. Asked me what kind of man I'd sent to his patch." He paused, and when Jock stayed silent, asked, "You wanna know what I told him?"

Jock nodded and gave it to him. He was more than curious about that conversation. "Yeah, boss. I do."

"Only the best." Mason pointed his finger at the camera, and Jock felt a phantom poke in his chest. "That's what I told him. Only the best. Don't prove me wrong." He heaved out a sigh and tipped his chin down. "We'll see you in a few days, brother. Call or text when you're on your way."

"Will do." Stunned by Mason's statement, that was all he could choke out.

Gunny turned to look at Mason, and Mason's head dropped back as he heaved another heavy sigh. "Fuck no, I won't make you give him a beatout. What the hell do you think, Gunny? What the fuck?"

The video disconnected and Jock locked his phone, shoving it deep in his pocket with a sigh.

He softly echoed Mason's words, the wonder heating his chest making his words sound rough and gritty. "Only the best."

***

Silly

Tired and hungry, and already anticipating the video chat she and Jock had planned for later that night, Silly parked her car in front of the apartment and swung out, not taking time to look around the lot before she headed to her front door. She'd been in the shop for more than fourteen hours, and lunch had been half a sandwich nearly ten hours in the past, so all she wanted to do was bolt some food and then veg on the couch until Jock called. So it was a surprise when she heard a man's voice call her name. "Silly, hey."

Key in the lock, she turned to find a man she vaguely recognized from the IMC blowout standing about three feet away. "Yes?" No matter that she knew who he belonged to, she took the cautious route, removed the key without turning it, and threaded her keys between her fingers. Her guns were in the apartment, her knife in the car. Without anyone at her back, the makeshift knuckles would have to do if something bad came out from whatever this was.

He frowned and executed a long step backwards, giving her another couple feet of space. "Hey, honey, didn't mean to take you by surprise. Just wanted to chat."

"The shop has a phone. Not even cups on a string, it's real and shit, even has voice mail." She told him the same thing she would have said to Slate, or Bones, and like those men, he grinned at her sass. "If it was important and I wasn't there, which I was all day, they could have called my cell."

"Wanted to chat face-to-face." He paused, tipped his head to one side, and she didn't know what to do with the flare of annoyance that crossed his face. "You don't know who I am, do you?" Silly shook her head, and he gave her a chin lift as he declared his name. "Wildman."

"Pleased. Now back to what you wanted?" She shifted her weight and saw he noted it, giving her another tiny frown. "Wildman?"

"Your man's RWMC." He stated something still true, so she gave him that and nodded. "I'm IMC."

"Clued in on that from your cut." She shook her head. "Seriously, what do you want, Wildman? I'm tired, I'm hungry, and I want to sit down."

"Easier for me to show you. And then we'll take it inside." It was her turn to frown at his self-declared invitation, because he didn't come in her direction at all but turned and waved at a truck down the way. A woman climbed out and turned towards them as she shut the door. The first glimpse of her face made Silly's breath catch in her throat. She didn't have to see him to know he was grinning broadly when he muttered an introduction that wasn't an introduction. "My woman."

Silly smiled big at the carbon copy of Mason walking her way.

***

Jock

Ass to the floor of the porch, he leaned back against a post, angled so he could see Gunny and Sharon lounging on the swing but still be able to glance out over the lake. Jase, DeeDee, Tyler, Jonny, and the rest of their crew of kids were in the water, Cade, Kitten, and even little Josh paddling around them, heads held up out of the water by vests and other floaties. Tank padded along the edges of the water restlessly, his groans of unhappiness able to be heard over the shouted laughter of the kids. Gunny's dogs were tired from earlier swim time and lay in the dirt along the path to the water, tails and paws jerking in doggie dreams.

"You're sure about this?" Gunny's gruff question came again, something like the tenth time he'd asked. "You check out the VA down there? Got a doc lined up?"

Jock kept watching Jase as he lifted Josh high, then dropped him into the water, catching him just as he hit and keeping the boy from dunking entirely under the water. Tank chewed on a bark, the sound coming out like an old man's grumble, subsiding when Jase acknowledged the dog with a look. Jock smiled and nodded. "Yeah. Ace, he's a founder for the Caddo Hobos, he hooked me up with his doc's info. Sounds like a good guy, a lot like what we've got in Bulldog. I called yesterday to have my files transferred down. I'm covered. It should be good, brother."

"It fuckin' well better be." Gunny's grumble came out as if it had been pushed through gritted teeth, and the comparison between his irritated and anxious tone and how Tank sounded didn't escape Jock. He stifled the grin that caused and nodded again. Silence for a moment, then more grumbling. "How the fuck is my boy gonna know his uncle, you move down there?"

Jock twisted his neck to see Sharon smiling fondly up at her husband, head on his shoulder, body sprawled across his much like Silly had been on Jock only weeks ago. She was showing, just barely, her belly softly rounded. Still, Gunny's hand rested protectively across where his son was growing.

Right here was where Silly had forced the discussion about kids, something Jock hadn't forgotten, and he made a vow right there to bring her back here when she was carrying, re-create the moment, and let them bask in the knowledge that their love hadn't faltered one iota.

"I'll be back up here to visit." He shrugged. "And you'll be down to see Vanna. It's not a far jump along the Gulf to come and see me." He leaned forwards, looped his arms around his knees, and told Gunny seriously, "I'm not about to lose the brother who saved my life. You and me, we're tight, and distance ain't gonna fuck that up, man."

"It better goddamned well not, or I'll fuckin' kill you."

"Gunny," Sharon interjected, voice shaking with laughter. "That'd kind of make it a moot point."

"I don't fuckin' care. He knows what I mean." Gunny hadn't taken his eyes off Jock, and the glare intensified as he muttered, "Best man I ever met, sittin' right here on my goddamned porch, and him about to take that goodness down and spread it along the coast. You straighten up their shit, you hear me?"

"Are you really tellin' me that shit?" Jock knew his voice was disbelieving, but then again, he knew all the Rebels, and with the qualities Mason and Slate, Jase, Bones, and all the others brought to the table, there was no way Jock would believe himself worthy of that title.

"Best goddamned man I ever met," Gunny shot back firmly and lifted his chin, resting it on the crown of Sharon's head as he clipped off another word. "Truth."

Sharon smiled, then that spread to a grin, and after a dramatic pause, she made both men laugh loud and long when she muttered, "Hashtag fact."

***

Mason

Sitting stock-still, he listened to the silence from the other end of the phone call for another moment, then annoyed at being put in this position at all, restated his demand, forcing out between clenched teeth, "You get me?"

"Oh, I get what you think you can fuckin' feed me, but what you gotta know is you don't have a fuckin' thing to do with any fuckin' thing in my club. But I get what you're sayin', that much I do get." The words were bitter and clipped, driven from a man who ran a dominant club managing a dozen relationships every day, and now angry at being made to concede anything. There was a long pause that Mason allowed to linger, then he heard a grudging, "Brother."

"Just sayin', he's been not just an asset, but a friend. I've got brothers, and we both know how that is under the patch. And then I've got *brothers*"—he placed subtle emphasis on the word—"and you feel that, too. I know you do." Mason leaned back in his chair, staring at the pictures Willa had on his office walls. He'd made certain to be at home for this call, not that Twisted knew that fact, but in Mason's mind, it meant his ask was personal. "He's solid, break his back for the ones who matter, and that means every fuckin' brother under the patch. Man's got a handful of friends, and he needs them. Give him that, Twisted.

Give him that there, keep him solid—and that marker you think I hold over you, that shit is gone."

Predictably argumentative, Twisted shot back, "Ain't wipin' a marker to take a man on who's worth it."

Jesus. This man couldn't take a gift if it was thrust into his hands. Mason schooled himself to patience, holding to the knowledge Twisted ran a tight club with little attrition, meaning his men came and stayed, lifers. "And I told you I wasn't holdin' a marker for ridin' alongside you when it was my goddamned sister needed rescue." Mason snorted, the remembered argument that night memorable, now legend in the bayous. "Not that you fuckin' listened to me then, either."

"She was taken from my clubhouse, brother. Under my watch, out from under my men, drugged and hauled out, stranded in the middle of the fuckin' woods. That's worth more than a marker, but I was pleased that's all you took."

"Sh—"

"And yeah," Twisted barreled on, "I get that you didn't want even that, but you gotta give me it, man. My clubhouse, my men, my watch. Penance, man. That shit calls for blood, and you know it."

He was right, something Mason found hard to acknowledge. Silence again stood between them until Mason finally gritted out a noncommittal, *"Fucker."*

"Ayeap." It was Twisted's turn to snort a laugh. "You talk to her lately?" Mason made a vague noise, and Twisted kept talking. "She's a fuckin' nut, man. Hooked too damn tight to Wildman, she's here every goddamned weekend. That pair done broke two goddamned beds. I finally told the man to get his own place, because we didn't wanna hear that shit every goddamned weekend."

Gut slowly rolling, Mason groaned. "Fuck, man. I do *not* need to know my sister's gettin' her freak on." It was quiet for a moment, then he asked softly, "She's good, though? When you see her? Jussy's good?"

"Yeah, she's good." Mason could hear the humor in Twisted's gentle voice and smiled at that evidence of truth. "Won't be long and she'll be relocating, too. My ask is that she not bring an echo of the feds with her when she comes. Wanna know what she said to that?"

"I bet it wasn't what you expected."

"Nawp, it wasn't. She told me the feds would be so glad to get shut of her, they'd offered her a buyout of her house. I don't think she'll be missin' them much, either. Asked her what she'd be doin' for a job, and get this, the woman's thinkin' of openin' up as a PI. Can you imagine that shit?"

"She'd be good at it." Mason shook his head. "Wildman's got his hands full with her, that's certain."

"No shit, Sherlock." Twisted laughed outright, and Mason grinned at the sound. "No shit."

Time to wind this up. "Alright, back to Jock. You got him, right? Nothing's gonna go sideways at the last minute?"

"I got him, brother. He's mine to sponsor, don't matter what Wildman wants or says, and I'm IMC so that shit's locked down tight." There was a sound in the background, and Twisted grunted, then muttered, "Fuckin' shit. Gonna hafta let you go, man. I got Ace in my house, and he's lookin' POed."

"Good talk, brother." Mason didn't wait for Twisted's response, ending the call.

He stared up at the pictures for a moment longer, then shouted, "Willa, when's supper, woman?"

Faintly through the door, he heard his loving wife's response and couldn't have stopped his laughter if he'd tried.

"Bite me, big man."

Rebels and IMC

Jock

Gunny pressed a knife into his hand. "Do it how you want, but be respectful." He and Jock stood in front of the entire Fort Wayne membership, the room quiet but for random sounds of shuffling boots or a cough. "Respect the patch."

"Always have," Jock told him, voice coming out rough as he swept the faces around him with his gaze. "And always will."

It took about four minutes to clip through the multitude of threads holding his hard-earned center and two rockers to the leather. He didn't do a neat job, didn't try to pull the ends through or smooth over the holes and hide them. He wanted them to know this mattered, and to know that he'd be thinking of this act every time he put the vest on for a long time.

Patches stacked on the bar top, he folded the blade back into the handle before returning it to Gunny.

His friend had been mutely supportive throughout, first standing at his back when he talked to the officers, then standing at his back when approached by irate members, and still standing at his back now, as Jock performed one of his final acts as a Rebel Wayfarer member.

"Still plannin' on leavin' in the mornin'?" Gunny laid a hand on Jock's shoulder, fingers digging deep. "You're sleeping at my place tonight. Don't even think about arguin'. Cade, Kitten, and Josh all need their Uncle Jock time before you go." He rattled Jock's bones. "Give Sharon a minute with Tankster, brother. Goodness all around."

Unable to speak, Jock nodded, because he wanted that, too.

"They don't do right by you, you call me." Gunny's voice had turned rough, shot through with pain. "I'll kick their asses."

Jock nodded again, knowing that call would never be made. Silly made any cost worth it, and he was locked in to the decisions made. Still, the constant refrain in his head these past days had been one of disbelief. Leaving the Rebels felt disloyal on so many levels, even going with the multitude of blessings from officers, brothers, and friends. He thought of Silly, the flash of her smile, the hope in her eyes the last time he'd seen her. *Not disloyal.* He swallowed hard. *Because of what they did for me, what they are to me, I'll always be a Rebel.*

He needed to give Gunny something, had been holding it for a while, and decided he'd never have a better opportunity than this. "You saved me, you know." Gunny stilled, and silence grew in a circle around them as men's conversations fell away. "All of you. You saved me. Took me into the fold as if I'd always been here. Gave me something to hold to every day, believed in me, offered me a goal to work towards when I needed it most. If you, any of you, ever have a need, you call me." Gunny's heavy hand clutching at his shoulder was all the response he needed.

Four days later he pulled up at the small house Silly had rented with an option to buy. He'd seen pictures, taken a video tour with her, but in person the place was even more gorgeous than he'd expected. The sprawling acre of grass around it would be a bitch to mow, but it had room for Tank to romp as much as the old boy could romp. The house had three bedrooms, and he hadn't said anything to Silly about it, but he was already planning a nursery in his head. No man and woman couple alive needed three bedrooms, unless it was to grow their couplehood into a family.

She burst from the front door as he was climbing out of the pickup, leaving his door hanging open behind him so the dog could follow him down. This meant he had time to round the front of the truck and catch Silly as she threw herself at him, arms around his neck, legs around his waist. He cradled her round ass in one hand as he met her mouth with his, overwhelmed by a feeling he hadn't had in a while. *I'm home.*

***

Jock stood in the clubhouse of the Incoherent MC's Hammond chapter, watching as a sea of upraised thumbs guaranteed him a brotherhood.

True to his word, after a lengthy argument with Twisted, Wildman was his sponsor, a relationship they'd have for life, even after Wildman's responsibilities ran out in six months. Arm stretched up and around his shoulder, Wildman pulled him to the center of the bar and pushed and pulled until Jock was positioned where he wanted with the IMC flag on display behind them. "Take a picture," Wildman called out as the outside door opened, sunlight following the women flooding in from outside, given the word that business was done.

Silly stood directly behind a woman, and once he pulled his gaze off his ole lady, he focused in on her. Dark hair, grey eyes, wide, firm jaw. She was the female version of Mason, and had to be Justine. She lifted her phone, gave Wildman a wink, and snapped off several pictures. "Got it, baby," she called, and Jock startled, because even her voice held echoes of Mason's.

"That, my friend," Wildman muttered, "is my woman."

Jock held out his other arm and watched Silly head his way, gold glints from her brows and ears, color on her bare neck and shoulders, and color in her hair, held back today with a bandana that proudly proclaimed her an IMC supporter.

"And that, my friend," he returned, "is mine."

~ ~ Fini ~ ~

THANK YOU SO MUCH FOR READING
Going Down Easy!

I truly hope you enjoyed this crossover story tying things together even tighter between the Rebel Wayfarers MC and the Neither This Nor That MC sagas. Thanks for takin' this trip along with me.

~ML

ABOUT THE AUTHOR

Raised in the south, *Wall Street Journal* & *USA TODAY* bestselling author MariaLisa learned about the magic of books at an early age. Every summer, she would spend hours in the local library, devouring books of every genre. Self-described as a book-a-holic, she says "I've always loved to read, but then I discovered writing, and found I adored that, too. For reading...if nothing else is available, I've been known to read the back of the cereal box."

Want sneak peeks into what she's working on, or to chat with other readers about her books? Join the Facebook group! **bit.ly/deMora-FB-group** deMora's got a spam-free newsletter list she'd love to have you join, too: **bit.ly/mldemora-newsletter**

~~~~~

My Rebel Wayfarers MC and the Neither This Nor That MC series do cross over, along with the Occupy Yourself band books, so readers have a couple of choices. The series can be read independently beginning with RWMC, OYBS, and then NTNT without too many spoilers. There's also a crossover between my RWMC world and Lila Rose's Hawks MC world. Or they can be read intertwined—in chronological order.

Here's the recommended reading order if you want to follow according to timing:

Mica, RWMC #1
A Sweet & Merry Christmas, RWMC #1.5
Slate, RWMC #2
Bear, RWMC #3
Born Into Trouble, OYBS #1
Jase, RWMC #4
Gunny, RWMC #5
Mason, RWMC #6
Hoss, RWMC #7
This Is the Route of Twisted Pain, NTNT #1
Harddrive Holidays, RWMC #7.5
Duck, RWMC #8
~~~~~

Biker Chick Campout, RWMC #8.5
Watcher, RWMC #9
Treading the Traitor's Path: Out Bad, NTNT #2
Living Without, Lila Rose's Hawks MC: Caroline
     Springs #4
Shelter My Heart, NTNT #3
A Kiss to Keep You, RWMC #9.25
Gun Totin' Annie, RWMC #9.5
Secret Santa, RWMC #9.75
Trapped by Fate on Reckless Roads, NTNT #4
Bones, RWMC #10
Gunny's Pups, RWMC #10.25
Not Even A Mouse, RWMC #10.75
Road Runner's Ride, RWMC #12.5
Never Settle, RWMC #10.5
Fury, RWMC #11
Christmas Doings, RWMC #11.25
Gypsy's Lady, RWMC #11.5
Thunderstruck, NTNT #5
Going Down Easy
No Man's Land
Cassie, RWMC #12

~~~~~

Also by MariaLisa deMora

Neither This Nor That MC

romance series

Legends are born from moments like these. Folktales spun around a single point in time so
~~~~~

perfect, you can almost hear the click resonating through the universe as things align. Meet Twisted, Po'Boy, Retro, and Ragman, good old boys from southern states who have many things in common. First, is a bone-deep love of the biker lifestyle. Second, would be their love of the brotherhood, and knowing that you trust the man at your back. Finally, these men have the love of a good woman. None of these come without a price, and it is our pleasure to journey along with them as they discover the blessings that can be won, and lost along the way.

> *This is the Route of Twisted Pain*
> *Treading the Traitor's Path: Out Bad*
> *Shelter My Heart*
> *Trapped by Fate on Reckless Roads*
> *Thunderstruck*

5-Star Reviews for the stories of the NTNT MC series

This is the Route of Twisted Pain
"This is the Route of Twisted Pain is an exhilarating, gripping romance novel contrived of incredible world building, complex yet relatable characters, and a unique, captivating plot.

Gifted storyteller MariaLisa deMora beautifully balances exciting suspense, fast action, intriguing secrets with delicious, blazing hot romance scenes. Readers will be up all night with this riveting page-turner."
~ NY Literary Magazine

I am completely tickled in my fancy for TWISTED! First off, let me state that there was one thing I didn't like about this book and that is the LAST PAGE! I hated for it to end. I dearly loved this book and its characters as well as their setting.
~Colleen M.

Gripping tale
Twisted and Penny fit together beautifully. The book covers so much more than just their love story. Great introduction to the Incoherent MC. The tale is gripping and gritty. The journey is full of twists and turns that keep you on the edge of your seat. I couldn't put it down. Cannot wait for the next one.
~Lillmil

Twisted is one of the most original and interesting characters I have read in a long time. Marialisa's character building is setting a high bar for her to follow, she will hopefully continue with Po'Boy's story. The Route of Twisted Pain was pure brilliance, and I highly recommend this read.
~Penny T.

This book obsessed me!
This may be the best book I read all year.
These people...they're not characters, they're real...
have stuck in my head from the day I met them.
MariaLisa deMora can throw words down that'll
Twist (hehe) your insides up till you can't breathe
for waiting to hear what's next!
I'm working my way through her other 'families' and
yup....she really is that good.
~DeLane

Treading the Traitor's Path: Out Bad
"Treading the Traitor's Path: Out Bad is a solidly
engrossing, well-written novel by a talented author.
MariaLisa deMora delivers a thrilling ride filled with
exciting suspense, deliciously explicit, vivid sex
scenes, and gritty, fast-paced action. Her characters
are smart, complex, and strong with sharp edges.
The settings meticulously detailed.
Fans of Motorcycle Club romance stories will not
want to miss this second installment in deMora's
exciting series."
~ NY Literary Magazine
What an amazing read! DeMora does not simply
wrote a book, she pulls you into a different world.
When you read her work, you are very much
surrounded by the characters and setting. Prepare
for a book hangover because once you finish the
book, you will still be stuck with Po Boy.
~KW

THIS WAS AMAZING. Highly recommend for a good story line, interesting characters. I just wish there was more more more.
~Laura

Loved This Book!
What did I just read?! Is my kindle still working? I'm pretty sure it combusted into flames while reading this story. RED HOT READ for 2017. Not what I was expecting at all! I tend to stay away from ménage a trois, because for me it's hard to say there's any kind of conflict except for jealousy, and the ending kind of leaves things unresolved and unrealistic. NOT THIS BOOK! The best one out there guaranteed.
~Linda A

...seriously this series is just WTF so freaking good. Dark, Twisted, harsh, painful and raw. Po'Boy lives for his club, his brothers and his family, there is nothing he wouldn't do for them.
~Fay

I live and breathe for books like this! Fabulously Naughty!...Wickedly Hot! This is my first book by MariaLisa deMora and it will not be my last. MariaLisa delivered a 5 STAR READ! The plot is filled with action, suspense, romance and tons of hot scenes.
~Jenny F

~~~~~
~~~~~

Alace Sweets, a dark romantic suspense standalone

A dark thriller, this book is not a light read. Filled with edge-of-your-seat suspense, this intense story commands the reader's attention as it drives towards the explosive ending. Alace Sweets is a vigilante serial killer, with everything that implies and is sure to trip all your triggers. Be ready.

At seventeen, Alace Sweets turned a corner in her life, taking the wrong shortcut home from school.

Resisting the harsh knowledge her attackers will never be made to pay for their actions, Alace takes a stand. Justice must be served, and if fate's scales are out of balance, she's determined to set things right as best she can.

When the laws of men fail, the rules of Alace prevail.

5-Star Reviews for Alace Sweets

"Whatever deep dark trench [deMora] pulled a character like Alace from should be revisited again and often."
~Confessions of a Serial Reader

"deMora has a superb story-line and exceptional character development. All of her characters have such depth that will intrigue the reader..."
~Turning Another Page

"Hot, sweet, dark thriller."
~Beth D

"It will keep you on the edge of your seat and give you chills."
~Escape Reality Book Blog

"Disturbing, haunting, sickly; yet hot, sexy and heart racing!"
~Amanda L

"From the first page [deMora] pulls you into the world she has created and you do not even try to escape..."
~Little Shop of Readers Blog

"A must read for all those dark, gritty romance fans out there."
~Sweet & Spicy Reads

"You will find yourself so drawn into the story that the outside world is blocked out and your locking the doors and turning on all the lights."
~Danena F

"Don't judge me for bonding with a vigilante serial killer, she's more than what she does."
~iScream Books

"Thrilling...chilling...full of suspense, nail biting edge of your seat excitement."
~Tracey H

"Every time MariaLisa deMora picks up her pen (or opens her computer), she creates characters you want to believe in."
~Gail S

"Intriguing dark storyline, beautiful love story and nail-biting conclusion, what more could a reader ask for?"
~Manda M

"This book takes you a dark and twisted ride that is gripping..."
~Renee Entress' Blog

"This book is dark and gritty and I literally had to take a day off from reading it because it's that intense."
~My Girlfriend's Couch

"This is my favourite book so far from this author …
I recommend this book if you enjoy dark romantic
thrillers."
~Cheekypee Reads and Reviews

"There's not enough stars to give this book and 5
just doesn't really do it justice!"
~DeLane C

"I couldn't put this book down from page one! Tried
to stop & go to bed but couldn't sleep thinking
about Alace and got up & finished the book."
~Debbie M

"MariaLisa DeMora, wordsmith that she is, made
this a story of the enlightenment of a woman and
finding love in a life where she has had none."
~Kat W

~~~~~

Hard Focus, a criminal thriller standalone

This is an intense page-turner, a gut-punch twist-filled story about a woman who has confidence in herself, believes she's a good judge of character, and has filled her life with people she can trust. She's right, but she's also very, very wrong. Readers
~~~~~

will have a time of it trying to decide who to watch closest.

Where do you place your trust when your own instincts betray you?

Connie Rowe is a receptionist at a respected legal firm. She's a little bit sassy, a lotta bit happy, has good friends, and is adored by her neighbors.

Life is good.

She's got a boyfriend she enjoys spending time with. He can be a little intense, but he's got a lot going on in his own life, sorting out his young daughter and nightmare of an ex.

Life is grand.

"Trust your gut." That's what Connie's police officer father told her often, training his daughter to believe in herself through the years.

But … what happens when you can't? When your intuition lies?

What happens when things come into Hard Focus?

5-Star Reviews for Hard Focus

"Hard Focus is one very well-written tale. 5 stars is not enough for me."
~Tabitha

"What a powerful story. [deMora] kept me invested from the first word to the last."
~Jesse R

 "I strongly recommend this book for both entertainment and to broaden your knowledge of certain laws that must be revisited."
~Words Turn Me On

"A intense page turner. Once you start, you can't put the book down."
~Tracey H

"A beautifully written, powerful read that I can't rate highly enough. This story will stay with me always."
~Gayle

"[deMora] has a certain magical touch to writing her characters, that they become either your nemesis, your best friend, or your love interest. That is certainly portrayed in this spin around. Loved it, loved it, loved it."
~Sandy K

"Wow! I am in awe of deMora's skill in crafting this story."
~Kat W

"I keep sayin that there just aren't enough stars to give to some of Marialisa deMora's books…this one is no different!"
~deLane

"Where do I start with this one…I read this in 3 1/2 hours uninterrupted, I absolutely could NOT put it down. Very deep, keeps you guessing, what's gonna happen next, kind of book. I love how strong her characters are, especially the females!"
~Wendy I

"Sometimes I feel like MariaLisa deMora is the one I should be watching out for. I started reading her books because I'm addicted to MC Romance, but then she decides to change things up and I just follow her wherever she leads me like a Pied Piper. I never know what to expect, and sometimes I'm afraid to find out, but it's always an adventure."
~Rosa for iScream Books Blog

"A plot full of twists and turns, a story that's not quite what it seems, strong characterization, jaw dropping revelations… what more do you need from a book?"
~Manda M

"This book had twists I didn't see coming. Loved it!"
~Lori R

 "This book kept me turning the pages wondering what was going to happen. I am usually pretty good at guessing twists but not with this book. She totally surprised me and brought me out of my funk. 5 stars."
~Glenna M

"What an amazing story! Filled with a smidge of suspense, a dash of action and a heap of realism of our country's laws and how their vague application to victims can adversely affect its citizens and the people in their lives."
~Naughty Mom Story Time

ADDITIONAL SERIES AND BOOKS

Please note that books in a series frequently feature characters from additional books within that series. If series books are read out of order, readers will twig to spoilers for the other books, so going back to read the skipped titles won't have the same angsty reveals.

Rebel Wayfarers MC series:

Mica, #1
A Sweet & Merry Christmas, #1.5
Slate, #2
Bear, #3
Jase, #4
Gunny, #5
Mason, #6
Hoss, #7
Harddrive Holidays, #7.5
Duck, #8
Biker Chick Campout, #8.5
Watcher, #9
A Kiss to Keep You, #9.25
Gun Totin' Annie, #9.5
Secret Santa, #9.75
Bones, #10
Gunny's Pups, #10.25
Never Settle, #10.5

Not Even A Mouse, #10.75
Fury, #11
Christmas Doings, #11.25
Gypsy's Lady, #11.5
Cassie, #12
Road Runner's Ride, #12.5

Occupy Yourself band series:

Born Into Trouble, #1
Grace In Motion, #2 (TBD)
What They Say, #3 (TBD)

Neither This, Nor That MC series:

This Is the Route Of Twisted Pain, #1
Treading the Traitor's Path: Out Bad, #2
Shelter My Heart, #3
Trapped by Fate on Reckless Roads, #4
Thunderstruck, #5

Rebel Wayfarers & Incoherent MC (NTNT) crossover stories:

Going Down Easy
No Man's Land

Mayhan Bucklers MC series:

Most Rikki-Tik, #1
Mad Minute, #2
Pucker Factor, #3
Boocoo Dinky Dau, #4

Borderline Freaks MC series:

Service and Sacrifice, #1
More Than Enough, #2
Lack of Inbetween, #3
See You in Valhalla, #4

If You Could Change One Thing:
Tangled Fates Stories

There Are Limits, #1
Rules Are Rules, #2
The Gray Zone, #3

Other Books:

With My Whole Heart
Alace Sweets
Hard Focus
Dirty Bitches MC: Season 3

More information available at **mldemora.com**.